"What are you doing here?"

"Saving you frked around at th[...]han slumped on [...]ard her, closing t[...]n in a stride.

Sara didn't protest when he pulled her into his arms. In fact, she melted against him.

"It's okay, sweetheart. You're all right now," he soothed as he folded her close. There was nothing wrong with comforting her, he told himself. Then he'd let her go.

He thought he had himself under control... until the feel of her feminine body, the smell of her familiar scent, the touch of her breasts pressed against his chest chased all rational thought from his mind.

No matter what her involvement, no matter how guilty, she felt too good to let her go.

REBECCA YORK

USA TODAY bestselling author Ruth Glick published her one hundredth book, *Crimson Moon*, a Berkley Sensation, in January 2005. Her latest 43 Light Street book is *The Secret Night*, published in April 2006. In October she launches the Harlequin Intrigue continuity series SECURITY BREACH with *Chain Reaction*.

Ruth's many honors include two RITA Award finalist books. She has two Career Achievement Awards from *Romantic Times BOOKreviews* for Series Romantic Suspense and Series Romantic Mystery. *Nowhere Man* was the *Romantic Times BOOKreviews* Best Intrigue of 1998 and is one of their "all-time favorite 400 romances." Ruth's *Killing Moon* and *Witching Moon* both won the New Jersey Romance Writers Golden Leaf Award for Paranormal.

Michael Dirda of *Washington Post Book World* says, "Her books...deliver what they promise—excitement, mystery, romance."

Since 1997 she has been writing on her own as Rebecca York. Between 1990 and 1997 she wrote the Light Street series with Eileen Buckholtz. You can contact Ruth at rglick@capaccess.org or visit her Web site at www.rebeccayork.com.

43 LIGHT STREET

REBECCA YORK
From the Shadows

RUTH GLICK WRITING AS REBECCA YORK

HARLEQUIN®

TORONTO • NEW YORK • LONDON
AMSTERDAM • PARIS • SYDNEY • HAMBURG
STOCKHOLM • ATHENS • TOKYO • MILAN • MADRID
PRAGUE • WARSAW • BUDAPEST • AUCKLAND

If you purchased this book without a cover you should be aware
that this book is stolen property. It was reported as "unsold and
destroyed" to the publisher, and neither the author nor the
publisher has received any payment for this "stripped book."

ISBN-13: 978-0-373-36073-4
ISBN-10: 0-373-36073-8

FROM THE SHADOWS

Copyright © 2002 by Ruth Glick

All rights reserved. Except for use in any review, the reproduction or
utilization of this work in whole or in part in any form by any electronic,
mechanical or other means, now known or hereafter invented, including
xerography, photocopying and recording, or in any information storage
or retrieval system, is forbidden without the written permission of the
publisher, Harlequin Enterprises Limited, 225 Duncan Mill Road,
Don Mills, Ontario, Canada M3B 3K9.

All characters in this book have no existence outside the imagination of
the author and have no relation whatsoever to anyone bearing the same
name or names. They are not even distantly inspired by any individual
known or unknown to the author, and all incidents are pure invention.

This edition published by arrangement with Harlequin Books S.A.

® and TM are trademarks of the publisher. Trademarks indicated with
® are registered in the United States Patent and Trademark Office, the
Canadian Trade Marks Office and in other countries.

www.eHarlequin.com

Printed in U.S.A.

CAST OF CHARACTERS

Alex Shane—He was determined to do his job, until Sara Delaney stepped into the picture.

Sara Delaney—Alex was afraid to trust her, even when he remembered their shared past.

Lee Tillman—Was he dead or alive, a victim or a murderer?

Clark Hempstead—Would the police chief help Alex—or send him to jail?

Reid Delaney—Was he angry enough to kill Tillman?

Emmett Bandy—He owed Lee money. How far would he go to cancel the debt?

Lewis Farmer—Did the handyman know what had happened to Lee?

Billy Shane—Why did he hate his brother, Alex?

Dana Eustice—What did Lee's mistress know about his disappearance?

Tripp Kenney—The militia leader was Lee's neighbor and perhaps his enemy.

Callie Anderson—Was she Lee's victim?

Chapter One

It started out the way it always did for Alex Shane. Erotic and arousing. A dream from the time when life was good. He was in bed with Cindy, mouth to mouth, naked body pressed to naked body.

One of her arms circled his shoulder, and her fingers tangled in his hair, urging him closer, then closer still. His hand moved from the curve of her hip to the swell of her breast—and his own body tightened as he heard her indrawn breath, felt her nipple harden beneath his fingers.

Even while it was happening, he knew it was just a dream. The same dream. The one that grabbed him by the throat again and again and shook him like a wild animal wringing the life from its prey.

A strangled cry rose in his throat. A cry of denial and anguish. Of anger and loss.

"No," he moaned, trying to claw his way back to consciousness.

Yet he was helpless to stop the drama from unfolding the way it always did. Helpless to make it come out any differently—no matter how many times he was doomed to repeat the terrible day when everything had changed.

One moment he was kissing Cindy, stroking her silky flesh, staring into her passion-drugged eyes.

In the next moment, he was no longer on the bed with her. Instead, he was standing in the doorway, watching his wife writhe on their navy-blue sheets with another man. Another man who'd been so busy with Mrs. Alex Shane that nobody had heard the front door open—or the footsteps coming down the hall.

By the time the guy heard the husband's shout of anger, it was already too late. Too late for all of them. Him, Cindy and Chad Enders, one of his fellow Howard County police officers.

At least Alex hadn't fired the service revolver that had leaped into his hand. Murderous thoughts had filled his mind, choked off his breath. But somehow sanity had intervened. At the last moment, he'd realized that the betrayal in the bedroom wasn't worth spending the rest of his life in jail.

"No," he cried out again, the terrible image burning its way through the sensitive tissue of his brain. He wanted to turn off the obscene pictures from a year ago but he was trapped for eternity—doomed to repeat the worst moment of his life, like an actor who could never get his part right.

By force of will, he managed to shatter the dream into a thousand jagged shards. Suddenly he was awake, lying in a tangle of sheets, his muscles taut, his body slick with perspiration.

His gaze flicked to the windows. Above the wooden shutters that covered the bottom two-thirds of the panes, he could see the first faint streaks of dawn.

He needed to get up, to distance himself from the dream. Swinging his legs over the side of the bed, he stood on the cold floorboards, the morning air sending a shiver over his sleep-warmed skin. After several seconds, he knew he wasn't going back to sleep any time soon. Sighing, he decided that he might as well get up and face the day.

In the bathroom, while he waited for the shower water to heat, he peered into the bathroom mirror. His dark eyes were rimmed with red and his hair needed cutting.

When the bathroom began to fill with steam, he stepped under water as hot as he could stand. The biting spray helped to sweep the last of the fog from his brain.

He had just rinsed his hair when a jangling sound reached him above the roar of the water.

The phone. Who the hell was calling at this time of the morning?

He ignored the summons for several rings, then cursed as he shut off the taps, leaped out of the shower and headed for the bedroom, leaving a trail of water in his wake as he snatched the receiver from its cradle.

"Yeah?"

The response from the other end of the line was just as abrupt. "I need you over here right away," a brusque voice said without preamble. There was no, "Did I wake you?" or "Sorry to call so early."

"Good morning to you too, Lee," Alex answered, stepping onto the pile of newspapers he'd left beside the bed. They immediately turned soggy under his bare feet.

"I've got a problem," Lee Tillman, eccentric millionaire, landed gentry and all-around son of a bitch elaborated.

"At the crack of dawn?"

"Yeah, well, I'm leaving for a vacation in Nova Scotia. I've electronically transferred five thousand dollars to your account."

"You mean to Randolph Security?"

"To you personally."

"I'm working for Randolph. We're on retainer to chase down your numerous enemies, remember?"

"Well, I have some personal business. I want you to do something for me. At your chicken-manure billing rate, I've just bought fifty hours of your time," the voice on the other end of the line clipped out. "Starting right now."

"You drive a hard bargain, Lee. How about I give you twenty-five hours for that price?"

Alex waited through the expected curse, rubbing his hand over the dark stubble on his cheeks and chin.

"Get your butt over here."

"My butt's not dressed."

"Throw something on," Tillman commanded, then continued issuing orders. "Don't park on my property. Leave the car on that old road in the woods just past my turnoff. And come up along the riverbank. The front door will be unlocked."

"Want to tell me what's going on?"

"No."

"Somebody threaten you?"

"Just get over here."

Closing his eyes, Alex pictured the imperious look in Tillman's smallish brown eyes, the stubborn cant of his narrow jaw. The man was used to giving orders and having people say, "Yes, sir."

However, Alex had always suspected there was a wide streak of insecurity below the bluster, and this morning there was more than arrogance in the reedy voice. There was a serrated edge that Alex had long ago learned to read as fear. It sounded as if the man was in trouble. Alex said he'd be right there and hung up.

After looking down at the newsprint that was now sticking to his feet, he retraced his wet steps and dried off quickly in the bathroom. He didn't even take the time to shave. He merely pulled on briefs, sweatpants and running shoes, yanking on a Crab Claw restaurant T-shirt as he trotted downstairs.

After hesitating in the front hall, he sprinted toward the relentlessly blue kitchen that the owners of the sprawling old house had installed. He hated it, but not enough to turn down a six-month lease at rock-bottom prices.

Pouring some of yesterday's coffee into a plastic mug with a lid, he heated it in the microwave, then added a splash of milk—for nourishment.

Minutes later, he was heading down the long driveway in his Toyota 4Runner. If his mind hadn't been focused on Lee's message, he would have enjoyed the early-morning ride along Route 33. Mallards glided through the marsh on one side of the road, and as he crossed the bridge over Oak Creek, he spotted a couple of enterprising men already fishing. Farther down the river he could see a marina, with everything from work boats to luxury cabin cruisers moored at the piers.

Funny how a few years changed your perspective. He'd been born not ten miles from here. And he'd felt as if his first semester at the University of Maryland in College Park was a miraculous escape from the backwater of the universe. He'd planned to leave his rural roots behind forever. First he'd worked as a cop in Howard County and thought he was going to stay there forever. When seeing Chad Enders in the squad room had made his blood pressure rise, he'd quit the department to join Randolph Security ten months ago. He'd already worked with them on several cases, knew he liked the guys on staff, and liked the freedom of not having to do everything by the police manual.

Then the Lee Tillman assignment had come up a month ago, and he'd jumped at the chance to decompress in his old stomping ground. So now he was back home, trying to figure out the next move in his sorry personal life while Randolph Security paid him to discover who was after Lee Tillman's hide.

There were plenty of candidates. Starting with the president of the local Boosters Club who was angry that Lee wouldn't sell some of his real estate holdings cheap—to be used for soccer fields. And progressing to the owner of the Duck Blind at the corner of Main and Chestnut Streets, who was pissed off that Lee was raising his rent. Then there was Emmett Bandy, one of Lee's friends, who was in debt to the man for fifty thousand dollars—money he couldn't afford to repay.

Lee had told Alex about them—and a number of others. Yet Alex knew there was stuff the cagey bastard was holding back. The maneuver was maddening. Lee Tillman wanted protection, but he wasn't willing to come clean with the company he'd hired to do the job.

Typical, Alex thought with a snort. Lee had always been secretive. And, unfortunately, a month of discreet digging hadn't yielded anything worth a restraining order, let alone an arrest.

Rounding the next bend in the road, he slammed on his brakes. An early-morning crew was already at work repaving one side of the two-lane highway. Alex's hands tightened on the wheel as the traffic slowed. Ordering himself to relax, he took several sips of coffee while he waited for the traffic to flow in his direction again, then made up for the delay by pushing past the speed limit.

As ordered, he drove past the white brick gateposts with the name The Refuge grandly displayed on a brass plaque. He knew the entrance marked the beginning of a blacktop driveway that wound through artfully manicured woods set off by fading pink and white dogwoods and blazing red azaleas.

Instead, he took the next turnoff, jouncing along an old dirt road that petered out in a stand of trees. Opening the car door, he started to get out, then withdrew his leg quickly. The shiny carpet of green leaves beside the car looked innocent enough, but he knew better, having learned one of his earliest lessons in Maryland nature lore the hard way. If poison ivy were a cash crop, the state's financial future would be made.

Eyeing the ground, he held the door ajar with his left hand and pulled the car forward into a clear place. From there it was an easy hike through the woods for the next fifty yards, until the path narrowed into a thicket of black-berry canes.

Security work on the Eastern Shore wasn't quite like operating in the Baltimore area, he thought as he skirted the brambles, and climbed over the jagged rocks dumped along the shoreline to hold back the Miles River. Before stepping onto the manicured lawn, he paused to scuff dirt from his tennis shoes, then crossed to the driveway and peered through the garage window. A sporty Jaguar JX6 was parked inside, but the silver Lexus sedan, which Lee would have taken on an out-of-town vacation, was missing.

Had his employer already left—and paid a five-grand retainer before departing for his vacation? Not likely.

After climbing the three wide steps to the porch, Alex strode to the massive front door. As he pressed the brass bell, he peered through the five-foot-long section of leaded glass, expecting Lee to come marching down the hall.

Alex suppressed a surge of anger. Lee had summoned him at the crack of dawn. So where the hell was he?

As Lee had said, the door was unlocked. Inside, the

house was completely, eerily quiet, except for the ticking of the ornate grandfather clock along the left wall.

Most people who owned a mansion this large would have employed at least one live-in servant. Lee made do, however, with a middle-aged African-American woman and her daughter who came in during the day and stayed late for dinner parties, and a guy who did odd jobs for him.

"Lee?" he called, stepping past the formal living room. It was dark and silent, the shades drawn.

Alex looked toward the broad, curving staircase. The office was at the top of the landing. Surely, he thought, Lee would have heard him if he were up there. Guessing that the man might be on the back terrace, Alex headed down the marble hallway.

"Lee?"

Silence.

Feeling uneasy, Alex stepped into the kitchen beyond the butler's pantry. Lee loved to cook, and he'd provided himself with a kitchen that was a gourmet's dream, with a six-burner stove, two microwaves, granite countertops and a sink large enough to bathe a Labrador retriever.

Alex's mind was starting to play tricks now, and it was a relief not to stumble over a body laid out on the ceramic-tile floor. Stepping under a rack of copper pots, he checked the big sink. It and a dish towel were wet, and the electric coffeepot held warm brew. Through the French doors Alex scanned the long expanse of fieldstone terrace at the rear of the mansion. No Lee. With an exasperated sigh, he stepped into a hallway lined with a series of closed doors. A quick check of the first two rooms revealed what looked like guest bedrooms. The third door, however, opened into a room darkened by heavy velvet drapes. Alex found a light switch, then blinked as a series of bright lights snapped on, illuminating the room.

He gave a short laugh at what he saw. An art gallery, a very private gallery. Near the door was a three-foot-tall white marble statue resting on a pedestal. It was a graphic depiction of Leda and the Swan—the myth about the Greek god Zeus taking the form of a bird and then seducing a human woman.

The large, gilt-framed pictures on the walls were as explicit as the statue. One showed a naked couple on a narrow bed with satin sheets. The woman's hands were tied to the elaborate brass headboard.

Alex turned away only to have his gaze come to rest on a romanticized painting of two lesbian lovers lying together on a fur rug in front of a blazing fireplace.

Everywhere he looked, he found similar works of art, all of them sexual in nature. Prurient interest kept him standing there, taking it all in until he shook himself out of the trance.

There was one empty place on the wall. Moving closer, he saw a rectangle of paint that was darker than the surrounding wall. And a small hole indicated where a hook might have been driven into the plaster.

But the picture that had no doubt hung there was gone.

Interesting. Had Lee taken down one of the paintings? Or had someone else?

He looked around, seeing no evidence of the missing artwork—if the stuff in here could be called art. When he stepped from the room and closed the door, the images from the room behind him added to his growing feeling of uneasiness.

It seemed that Lee Tillman had been hiding some very kinky personality traits.

He cleared his throat, called out again, "Lee?"

When he got no answer, he took the stairs to the office on the second floor. The fifteen-by-twelve room with its floor-to-ceiling bookshelves behind the antique desk was empty. But there was something missing, he noticed almost at once: the oriental rug, which he remembered well because he'd thought it looked opulent enough for a sultan's palace.

It flitted through his mind that Lee could have sent it out to be cleaned while he was away on vacation. But then his memory zeroed in on a case his friend Cal Rollins had caught when they'd both been in the Howard County Police Department. A serial murderer had hit his victims over the head, then carried them out of the house rolled in their own rugs.

Yeah, a nice thick rug would make a damn good wrapper for a body, Alex thought as he found himself wondering what would happen if a crime team did a Luminol test. Would they find traces of blood on the walls or the floor? He'd once seen the walls and floor of a bedroom that looked perfectly clean come alive with the green glow of the chemical, highlighting a grisly attack on a pregnant woman who had been murdered by her lover. The murderer assumed he had scrubbed away the evidence before going bowling with the guys. The chemical test had shocked him into a confession.

Alex snorted. No doubt, testing for bloodstains was premature. Yet from his earliest days as a cop, he'd learned to trust his hunches, and he sensed that there was something wrong here—if for no other reason than Lee's urgent call less than an hour ago.

Turning toward the desk, Alex saw a thin, unsmoked cigar.

Would an aficionado leave a cigar lying out if he was going on a trip? Maybe if he was in a hurry.

Damn, where was Tillman?

Alex walked closer to a calendar pinned to the cork-board on the wall beside the closet door, and focused on today's date—May 22. In the rectangle was a notation that said "vacation." The trip Lee had mentioned. Although many appointments were listed for the first part of the month, there was nothing after today in either June or July. Had Tillman planned nothing after the end of May, or had he just neglected to note anything on the calendar?

Alex was about to go through the desk drawers, when a noise coming from outside stopped him. A car door slamming.

Certain it had to be Lee, he was surprised by the degree of relief he felt. Tillman might be a pain in the ass at times, but in his gruff way he had befriended Alex's family twenty years ago when they'd been in trouble. Alex's dad had gotten himself killed in a boating accident, and his mother struggled to support two children. She'd already been doing part-time domestic work for Lee, and he'd increased her hours and recommended her to several of his poker buddies. Alex had always suspected that the guy had also slipped her some cash to keep her solvent while she got on her feet, which was one of the reasons he'd taken this present assignment.

Still, that didn't mean he was at Lee Tillman's beck and call. There had to be limitations.

When Alex heard the front door open and close, he started across the office, prepared to make it clear there would be no more urgent appointments. But he'd only taken three steps when he froze, listening to the sound of heels clacking on the floor of the foyer.

They weren't from Lee's shoes, not unless Lee had started wearing high heels and taking quick, feminine steps. And they weren't the footsteps of Lewis Farmer, who did odd jobs around the place.

The clicking heels proceeded up the stairs—firm and sure of where they were going. Alex did a quick inventory of other possibilities. It couldn't be Lee's housekeeper, Adele, or her daughter, unless they'd taken to cleaning house in their Sunday clothes. But what about Dana Eustice, Lee's longtime mistress? She'd certainly have access to the house and probably a key.

He had only a few seconds to decide what to do. He could brazen out a confrontation or he could duck into the storage closet and find out who was marching up the stairs as if she owned the place.

He chose the closet. It was small and lined with shelves of office supplies and magazines, but there was enough room in the center for him to stand. He snorted softly at the five-year supply of *Penthouse* stacked on the shelf beside him, figuring it went with the art gallery downstairs. Leaving the door open a crack, he leaned back against the shelves and stood quietly in the darkness.

The high heels drew near, and a woman stepped into the office. From his hiding place, Alex had an excellent vantage point to look at her.

She was wearing large sunglasses, so he couldn't see all of her face. But to his discerning eye, she appeared to be in her mid- to late-twenties. Blond. Slender, but with curves in the right places. Five five. In her trim suit and cream-colored blouse that exposed a discreet but tantalizing amount of skin below her throat, she looked as though she was on her way to an office or a business meeting.

It wasn't Dana Eustice, who was closer to Lee's age.

The spike heels that had sounded so authoritative on the steps were the kind that made a woman's legs look sexy, although Alex had always figured they must be hazardous to navigation.

Her blond hair didn't exactly fit the business image. It was long and loose and fell to her shoulders in soft waves. Pausing, she took off her sunglasses and tucked them into her purse. As she passed close by the closet, he noted that her eyes were light.

A memory tickled at the back of his mind. He knew her from somewhere. But where?

A long time ago…when they'd both been a lot younger…

Even with the professional outfit, she didn't seem like Lee's usual kind of business associate. More like somebody he might hire as his personal masseuse. Alex scratched that thought immediately. She looked too wholesome to be a party girl, and she had a slim, zipper-type briefcase wedged between her right arm and her body. She stood holding her lower lip between her teeth as she surveyed the empty office.

He watched her shake her hair, then roll her shoulders, as though something was making her restless. He hoped to hell it wasn't some subliminal vibration he was giving off.

She served him up a couple of bad seconds when she turned to focus on the wall to her right. Was she looking at the calendar or the closet? As she stood with eyes narrowed, the breath froze in his lungs. Then, to his vast relief, she set the briefcase on the corner of the desk and pivoted toward the bank of file cabinets.

He was still trying to figure out where he'd met her before as she reached the last cabinet on the left, pulled open the third drawer and extracted one of the folders. Straightening, she gazed around the room again, her expression pensive. Then, with a sigh, she reached inside the vee neck of her blouse and adjusted a bra strap that must have slipped down when she'd bent to pillage the drawer.

Very nice. Alex thought, grinning as he watched her move her full breasts into their properly subdued place. The maneuver had an unconscious sexiness about it that he found extremely arousing. Not like the stuff in the art gallery downstairs. This was real. And vibrant. And innocent.

Vibrant…innocent….

Then it struck him like a bolt of lightning where he'd seen her before.

Sara. No last name. Just Sara. Grown from a sweet little high-school girl into a very appealing woman. But now that the memory had leaped into his mind, he felt as if he'd been poleaxed.

Emotions and images flooded through him. Muncaster Park at night. The grove of trees. The dark riverbank. One of the beer parties that had been the chief activity during his senior year in high school.

The usual gang was there. The tough boys and girls from St. Stephens High. And then a group of girls from the local Catholic school had stepped into the haze of cigarette and marijuana smoke polluting the night air. Girls who didn't know that they were in over their heads with this crowd.

They had a few beers, sticking together in their own little group. Then the alcohol had loosened them up. They started giggling and egging each other on, seeing who was brave enough to flirt with the bad boys from St. Stephens. One of them came up to him, acting seductive, only, he could see she didn't quite know how to pull off the moves.

He gave her his heartbreaker grin, offered her a beer and waited until she'd downed some of the contents. Then he asked if she wanted to join him in the back seat of his car.

She cast a triumphant look back at her friends, then came along. Past a couple of motorcycles, right into the den of the Big Bad Wolf. He was thinking that he'd use his well-practiced techniques on her, go as far as he could—hopefully all the way.

But one draft of her, and everything changed. He discovered innocence in her kiss. An edge of fear and a fresh summer sweetness.

Ruthlessly, he cut off the memory.

Sweet little Sara might have been in over her head all those years ago, but she certainly seemed to know what she was doing now.

Teeth clenched, he watched her pick up the briefcase and shove the folder inside. On her way to the door, she paused beside the desk, and he tensed as he waited to see her rifle through the drawers. Instead, she selected a peppermint from the dish beside her, unwrapped it and popped the candy into her mouth.

For a moment, she stood with the wrapper in her hand, staring at the trash basket. If she pitched it, Alex reasoned, she wasn't worried about who knew she'd been here.

After a slight hesitation, she rolled the paper up and stuffed it in her briefcase. Then she headed out the door, having been in the office, he guessed, for less than two minutes total.

He let the breath he'd been holding ease out of him.
Sara.

He knew nothing more about the girl—or about the woman she had become. Back in high school he'd wanted to find out more. But he'd stopped himself because he'd known that Alex Shane was no damn good for her.

Had she stayed sweet and nice, or had she metamorphosed into something else? Was she retrieving a folder Lee expected her to pick up—or was she stealing evidence of a crime?

And what crime? Murder?

One thing was certain, she'd known exactly which file drawer to open and what to take. And he was going to find out why.

Chapter Two

His hands clenched in frustration, Alex waited until he heard Sara descend the stairs before stepping out of the closet. As soon as the front door closed, he sprinted across the landing to a window. From there, he watched as she got into what looked to be a three- or four-year-old burgundy Dodge parked in front of the house. He muttered an oath when he realized the angle of the porch roof prevented him from seeing the license plate.

Did he have a chance in hell of catching her? Maybe—if she was heading into town, which would mean she would have to pass the work crew repaving the highway. Cursing Lee's order to park so far from the house, he barreled down the steps and out the back door, then tore along the edge of the river, making it to the truck in less than three minutes.

He backed down the dirt road at breakneck speed and reached the highway, pulling in front of a pickup and ignoring the angry shake of the driver's fist, as he headed east toward St. Stephens.

His luck and his reckless driving were rewarded when he spotted Sara's car near the front of the queue at the construction site. Determined not to let his quarry make a timely escape, Alex pulled onto the shoulder, leaned on the horn and raced past several cars.

The construction worker directing traffic flipped him a rude hand gesture as he squeezed back into line and zipped past. About a mile down the highway, he eased in two car lengths behind her.

Alex managed to move in behind her Dodge before the traffic light on Main Street. The license number was MOD270—one of those green-and-white Save-the-Bay plates with a heron and cattails.

He was right behind her now, no longer afraid of losing her. As the tension eased, his mind began to stray back to that night, back to the party.

It was a pleasant memory. Much better than the dream that had awakened him so early in the morning.

Even at eighteen, he'd known how to please a woman. How to arouse her. Thrill her. Make her willing to give him what he wanted—because she knew they were both going to have a very good time.

But this girl, who told him her name was Sara, had turned the tables, without even realizing what she was doing.

He remembered his emotions that night. He remembered thinking a few minutes after they climbed into the back seat of that car that he should send her back to her friends. But he simply couldn't let her go. Not without satisfying the need that was suddenly clamoring inside him.

Her kisses started out unsure and tentative. But the honeysuckle warmth of her mouth lured him to deepen the contact, to drink in that sweetness, to teach her how a man and a woman could please each other.

When he cupped her breasts, she'd stiffened and told him to stop. He did as she asked. But then he soothed away the protest with more kisses and soft, reassuring words. When she was warm and pliant in his arms, he gently stroked the sides of her breasts, going slowly, letting the heat build gradually. It wasn't long before he was slipping his hands under her T-shirt and unhooking her bra so he could play with her hardened nipples.

He brought her to the edge of control—and found that he was right there with her. He wanted to plunge inside her and satisfy the craving that vibrated through him.

But some unaccustomed little voice in his brain told him that he'd surely hate himself in the morning if he took her innocence. Because that innocence was never in doubt.

So he'd pulled her onto his lap, facing him, urging her down so that her sex was pressed to his, separated by only a few layers of clothing. Too many layers, his mind screamed. But he kept it that way, moving his hands to her hips, moving her body against his, the friction and the pressure taking him higher and higher until he heard her cry out, felt her body convulse above his—and felt her take him with her.

The innocence and the eroticism had left him shaky, and when her eyes had blinked open, he'd been at a loss for words, overwhelmed by an experience that he couldn't explain either to her or to himself.

He'd wanted to keep her with him and do it again. Be inside her this time. Start something long term with her. But he'd known that she didn't belong with tough and cynical Alex Shane.

When he saw the dreamy, heavy-lidded expression on her face, he knew that he was on the edge of doing something stupid.

So he made his voice brusque and told her she'd better go back to her friends before she got into real trouble.

Her eyes snapped open, and she gave him a wounded look.

"Go on."

At that, she scrambled out of the car so fast that she'd hit her knee on the door handle.

He'd never seen her again. Not until today.

The memory had his blood boiling. Again he ordered himself to cool down. He'd made assumptions about Sara long ago. He couldn't afford to do it now. Now he needed no rose-colored impressions. Only the facts.

And he was trained to get them.

He stroked the stubble on his chin, thinking about the cocky kid he'd been at eighteen and the man he was now. Back then, he'd been as innocent as the girl he'd kissed in that car. Not about sex, of course. He'd had that all nailed down. But about life. About the way the world worked.

He'd learned to play by society's rules, and he'd thought that was his ticket to the good life. Marriage and a family, and a house in the suburbs. Then Cindy had pulled the rug out from under him and he'd realized that his rosy vision of the adult world had no more substance than his adolescent fantasies.

He'd been tough and cynical in his youth. He was tough and cynical now. And as far as he was concerned, the woman in the car ahead of him was guilty of something until proven innocent.

She stayed in the business district for several more blocks, then turned right toward the southeast part of town, a hodgepodge of older houses mixed with newer ones. He discovered her destination was a white clapboard Cape Cod on Redbud.

When she disappeared inside, he drove down the street and pulled into a convenience-store parking lot. Around the side of the building, he climbed out of the SUV and opened the back, where he kept a number of props.

He took out a brown cap, pulled it over his face and shrugged into a matching brown jacket. Then he retrieved a box wrapped with brown kraft paper, which he used to block the lower part of his face. His body language completed the transformation as he ambled back to Sara's street, his knees and shoulders slightly bent, like a guy with hardly enough energy to haul himself around. For effect, he tramped up several walkways, checking the names on the mailboxes, comparing them to the label on the package and shaking his head as if in exasperation. The mailbox on the front of Sara's house said S. E. Delaney, 1224 Redbud. Her married name, or had she been Sara Delaney all those years ago?

He hadn't seen a ring on her finger. But she could be divorced.

So now he had her full name and address and license number. With that amount of information, he could get a good deal more.

As he stowed the props again and drove away, he was thinking that he'd have to figure out a way to arrange a meeting with S. E. Delaney. A casual meeting that would give her no clue about his real purpose. But first he'd have to do some checking on her.

He detoured through the restored eighteenth-century commercial area of town, with its art galleries, real estate offices, restaurants and old-fashioned hardware store. According to Mrs. Chess, the woman who cleaned his house a couple times a week, the business district had once been a sleepy strip that served the local residents. Ever since Alex had known the place, it had catered to the tourists who flocked to the area like the migrating ducks and geese that stopped off on their way north and south. The boxy, redbrick municipal center stood out among the older buildings like a civic bad joke.

He thought about dropping by to see Police Chief Clark Hempstead, to report Lee as missing. But he knew it was too early for that, especially when Lee himself had said he was going on a trip and his calendar noted that fact. Besides, the idea of Alex Shane voluntarily paying a call on the St. Stephens police chief was pretty funny.

Eleven years ago, he'd been into more than sex and beer parties. He'd been in and out of the police station. On all kinds of juvenile charges. Stuff that was a little heavier than drinking beer—like stealing cameras from tourists' cars.

Probably Hempstead would drop his teeth if he knew Alex Shane had become a cop. Well, an ex-cop now. But he was still in the business, still on the right side of the law—most of the time. Because he knew damn well that Randolph Security sometimes skated a fine line between legality and vigilante justice. When he'd first worked with them—on the Cal Rollins kidnapping—he'd been too uptight to fully appreciate their methods. Then, the shock of seeing Cindy in bed with another man had given him a whole new perspective on life. He'd wanted to stop playing by the rules and working for Cam Randolph had given him the breathing space he needed.

His musings were interrupted by a flash of movement at the edge of his vision.

Blond, wavy hair. A blue business suit. Those erotic high heels. The briefcase.

It was her. Sara Delaney. Big as life and twice as plain. Right there on the sidewalk.

Had she seen him? Followed him downtown?

Even as he dismissed that possibility, he was frantically looking for a parking space. Luckily, it was still early in the morning, and the tourists who frequented the kitschy little shops weren't yet out in force. He was able to pull in front of a real estate office. Real estate was one of the booming industries in St. Stephens, because people came over here from the other side of the bay looking for vacation or retirement property.

Climbing out of the 4Runner, he started back up the sidewalk, as if he was maybe going to stop at the new gourmet coffee shop.

Ms. Delaney shifted her briefcase under her arm as she stood on the sidewalk across from the Windsor Art Gallery. She glanced right, then left. The road was clear, so she started to cross.

Out of nowhere, he saw a pickup roar around the corner, heading directly for her.

Alex's reaction was swift and primal—a runner's sprint that brought him pounding along the pavement even as he shouted a warning. "Watch out!"

Sara had gone stock still in the middle of the street. The truck was still speeding straight toward her, and he realized with a sick feeling that the only thing he'd accomplished by shouting was to make sure she was no longer a moving target.

Putting on a burst of speed, he shot forward, grabbed her shoulders and yanked her backward toward the curb. She screamed as his hands closed around her, screamed again as the vehicle whizzed by, shaking them both in a backwash of wind and exhaust fumes.

Swaying, he managed to stay on his feet for another few seconds. But her body made him overbalance, and he fell to the pavement, taking her with him.

Any chance of catching the license number of the truck was gone. Or of taking in any details of the vehicle, for that matter. The truck and driver were simply a blur disappearing around the next corner.

The woman in his arms struggled to sit up, and he realized that the two of them were lying in the middle of Main Street. A very dangerous place to be, particularly if the guy made another pass at Sara.

She looked dazed as he dragged her to her feet, then took several steps back, out of the roadway. His own legs were shaky, and he propped his hips against the fender of a car, cradling her slender body protectively against his.

Past and present blended in a confusing swirl. Years ago he and Sara were in the back seat of a car, aroused, touching, kissing. And now Sara was in his arms again.

Her head drifted to his shoulder. Her hand opened and closed around his upper arm. She was trembling, and he still wasn't all that steady on his own feet. It wasn't just from the near-death experience. It was from holding this woman close.

The smart thing would be to turn her loose. But it wasn't something he was prepared to do—yet.

It was the most natural thing in the world to stroke his hand over the shiny waves of gold that crowned her head. In his arms, her body felt fine-boned and vulnerable.

"It's okay," he murmured knowing the reassurance was as much for himself as for her. When he'd seen that truck speeding toward her, his whole body had gone cold as ice. "Everything's okay."

His heart was pounding as he waited for her to draw away, but she stayed where she was, in his arms. And his hand seemed to have a will of its own as it stroked over her shoulder, down her back.

The few people on the street had no more substance than shadows. He and Sara might as well have been alone.

Long ago, with her, he'd teetered on the edge of doing something stupid. He might have done that now, might have turned his head and stroked his lips against the tender line where her hair met her cheek. But her voice intruded into the fog that had wrapped itself around his brain.

"The truck," she gasped out, craning her head in the direction of where the vehicle had disappeared.

He made an effort to remember why she was standing there in his arms. Clearing his throat, he asked, "You saw it?"

"At the last minute. But it was too late. I couldn't move. If you hadn't pulled me out of the way…" She drew back and stared as though finally focusing on him.

He looked into her eyes. They were blue—blue as… He was too numb to come up with anything poetic. Just startlingly clear blue. In the darkness that night so long ago, he hadn't known their color, and in Lee's office, he hadn't gotten a close enough look.

Her mouth opened, then closed again. Slowly, very slowly she pulled away from him, her eyes wary now.

"Are you all right?" he asked, hearing the thickness in his own voice.

"Yes." She gave no sign of knowing him. Probably the teenage incident had made less of an impression on her than it had on him. Probably she wasn't used to drinking and the beer she'd consumed had wiped his face from her memory.

"My briefcase," she said, turning.

The thought of her stepping back into the street sent a wave of reaction zinging through him. "Stay here. I'll get it."

RELIEVED BEYOND MEASURE that his dark eyes were no longer on her, Sara sagged against the car fender, feeling as though the ground had dropped away from beneath her feet.

Lord, it was Alex Shane, the guy who had—

With a grimace, she cut off the thought, unwilling to put a name to what had happened one night eleven years ago—because she couldn't let herself think about it now, couldn't let him figure out that the scene with him in the back seat of that car was blazed into her memory like a flaming brand.

He had retrieved the briefcase and was coming back with it. Being careful not to touch his hand, she reached out and collected her property.

She hadn't seen Alex Shane in years, although she *had* taken the trouble to find out that he'd left town. She'd also thought about him far too often. What was he doing back here in St. Stephens? Some perverse little demon inside her urged her to find out.

He looked different. More mature, more battered by life, and he wasn't exactly dressed for Main Street. Long ago he'd cultivated a studied casualness in his appearance, now he looked as if he'd slept in his clothing.

He said something that she didn't catch because she was concentrating on her thoughts.

"What?"

"Did I hurt you when I knocked you down?"

She took a quick inventory, feeling a twinge in her shin and shoulder. "I guess I'm probably bruised somewhere."

His voice was deeper now, but still the voice she remembered. She bent to smooth her skirt, which was now smeared with grit.

Put your girlish feelings away, she ordered herself. *Put them into a compartment until later.* With her head bent, she took a few seconds to tamp down her emotions. When she felt composed once more, she raised her face toward his. "Thank you."

Still, he must have seen something lingering in her eyes, because he ran a hand through his dark hair. "I guess I look like I spent the night down on the docks. But I'm not a beach bum, honest. I was out for an early-morning run. I thought I wasn't going to, uh, bump into anyone.'' With a disarming grin, he held out his hand. ''Alex Shane.''

She didn't want to touch him again. But it was going to look strange if she ignored the polite gesture. ''Sara Delaney.'' She clasped his hand briefly, feeling her skin burn, before pulling her arm back. ''You come downtown to run?'' she asked.

''Only early in the morning. It's safer than the shoulder of the road.'' He turned his hands palm up. ''What are you doing down here so early?''

She gestured toward the art gallery. ''I was delivering some papers to Al Windsor. And some damn fool wasn't watching where he was going.''

He cleared his throat. ''You should sit down and relax. The coffee shop on the corner is open early. Want to have a cup?''

No. No, not with you. Not with Alex Shane.

She tried to look at him as though she'd never seen him before. He'd been a heartbreaker as a teenager. Maturity had only added to his rough good looks. His features were lean, his jaw strong, and his lips hinted at remembered sensuality.

She'd known he was a guy heading for big trouble, and more than once she'd wondered if he'd ended up in prison. Apparently he was a free man. But he seemed as dark and dangerous as ever. His hair was barely combed, and his two days' growth of beard made him look like the beach bum he'd claimed not to be. His sweatpants and his Crab Claw T-shirt were faded but clean.

When she didn't answer his question, he said, ''The coffee's on me.''

A cup of coffee. She could handle that, it might satisfy her curiosity. Because she *was* curious.

"I'd better leave the papers for Al first," she heard herself saying.

"Right."

She shifted the briefcase in her hands and felt a stab of pain.

Alex must have heard her indrawn breath. "What?"

Turning her palm up, she stared at the skin and was surprised to find that the heel of her right hand was scraped raw.

"You need to clean that up."

"I'm fine."

"You don't want it to get infected. I've got a first-aid kit in my truck."

He was taking charge of the situation very quickly, just as he'd acted quickly when he'd snatched her out of the path of the speeding vehicle. And on that long-ago night when he'd swept her into a world of sensuality she hadn't known existed.

She took a step back. "You don't need to go to any bother."

"Stop protesting." He took her arm firmly.

There was a moment when she might have resisted. Instead, she let him lead her down the block to a Toyota 4Runner. It was only a few years old and very well maintained. The black exterior was clean and polished, and when he opened the passenger door, she saw that the leather seats were spotless.

It wasn't what she'd expected, although she couldn't have said precisely what she'd been picturing.

After a moment's hesitation, she climbed onto the seat but left the door open as he slid behind the wheel.

"I'm not going to abduct you."

"I didn't think you were," she answered quickly, then pulled the door shut. Immediately she felt closed in. Too aware of Alex Shane. Too full of memories of the last time they'd been in a car together.

She watched as he twisted in his seat and fumbled on the floor in the back, coming up with an unopened bottle of water. Then he reached across her to the glove compartment, where he retrieved a first-aid kit. After getting out several sterile pads, he unscrewed the top on the water bottle and moistened them.

"Let's see that hand," he said, reaching for it, cradling it in one large palm while he gently washed her reddened flesh.

Earlier he'd held her in his arms, and this shouldn't feel anywhere near as intimate. But right after he'd snatched her from the jaws of death, she hadn't known who he was. Now she was vividly aware of his flesh against hers, of his very masculine body inches away.

She focused on holding perfectly still and on not making a sound as he cleaned the scrape but when he dabbed on antiseptic, she winced.

His fingers pressed hers. "Sorry."

"It's the stuff, not you," she answered, keeping her head down, aware that she wasn't precisely speaking the truth.

But she felt his eyes on her and found she had to look up.

When their gazes collided, he drew his hand away.

They sat in silence for several moments before she opened the door, picked up her briefcase and stepped quickly down to the sidewalk again. Alex followed, locking the vehicle behind himself, then hurrying to catch up with her.

She reached the spot across from the Windsor Art Gallery and started to step off the curb, and suddenly felt as though she was standing in the crosshairs of somebody's rifle scope. Stopping, she clenched her teeth, trying to fight off the shiver that traveled over her skin. Back in the car she'd been too preoccupied with the man beside her to focus on the way her hand had gotten hurt. Now she re-lived the seconds of terror when she'd looked up and seen the truck bearing down on her.

The reaction was ridiculous, she told herself. Yet she couldn't halt the sudden dread.

"Are you okay?" Alex asked.

"Yes!" she answered, the syllable coming out high and sharp. Closing her eyes for a moment, she took a deep breath. "Sorry. I'm a little...off balance."

"I can understand why."

"Let me get rid of the papers so we can have our cof-fee," she answered briskly.

"Right."

Still she made no move to step into the street. It was almost a relief when he took her arm and guided her quickly across the traffic lanes. Stopping in front of the art gallery, she pulled a large manila envelope from her brief-case, then bent to slip it under the door.

As Alex fell in stride beside her again, she slid him a sideways glance. On the surface, he looked relaxed, yet she still sensed his tension. Did he remember her, after all, and not want to embarrass her by saying anything?

Her steps faltered, then she picked up the rhythm of her stride again, deliberately gazing at the duck decoys, swim-wear, seascapes and T-shirts in the shop windows as she passed.

Located on the eastern seaboard of Maryland, St. Ste-phens had been settled early by colonists from Britain. Many of the buildings in the downtown area dated back to the colonial period. Others were Victorian. They gave the streets an antique charm. For much of its history, the town's commercial life had centered around the seafood and fishing industry, until a bridge had been built across the Chesapeake Bay, connecting the Eastern Shore to the mainland. Then tourists had discovered the area's appeal.

For every business catering to locals, there were three others aimed at visitors. The coffee shop was one of the new additions. Later in the day it would be crowded. This early in the morning there were only a few other customers.

In the cool, dimly lit interior, both she and Alex ordered cappuccino from the man behind the counter. She knew his name. Blake Richmond. She'd gone to St. Catherine's High School with him. He hadn't been a good friend. But they knew each other, and he gave her a smile and a nod as she ordered.

After the coffee arrived, she found Alex eyeing the display of muffins.

"How about a couple of those?" he asked.

"I don't usually indulge in sweets for breakfast."

"You're entitled to a treat."

"I suppose you're right," she murmured.

"What's your pleasure?"

Pleasure. The way he said it was warm and carnal. No, that was just her own reaction to his voice. "Um... cranberry nut," she managed to say, hoping she didn't sound too breathy.

"What about if we get an apricot, too, and split them."

If she'd been with any other man, the offer would have sounded tempting. Coming from Alex, it sounded much too intimate. But she decided it was easier not to protest, particularly since Blake was watching them with interest. That was one thing about a small town: People were nosy.

Like her, she silently conceded. She'd always been curious about what had happened to Alex Shane. Now that she had a chance to find out, there was no harm in indulging that curiosity, she told herself firmly.

She picked a table by the window, as far from the counter as she could get. Seated across from her, Alex used a plastic knife to carefully split the muffins down the middle, then put two halves on each of their paper plates.

Picking up the apricot, he took a healthy bite.

Sara eyed the fruit-studded confections, then decided that letting the food go to waste was foolish.

After taking a bite of the cranberry muffin and a sip of coffee, she raised her eyes to his and casually asked, "So what's the respectable job that keeps you off the docks?"

He took another bite of his own muffin, chewed and swallowed, and she wondered if he was stalling for some reason.

Finally he answered, "I work for a company that does various types of security work."

"Like installing alarm systems?" Sara probed.

He shifted in his seat. "We do some of that. Plus evaluations. And we take investigative cases."

"In St. Stephens? You mean, like evidence for a divorce? Stuff like that?"

"I can't really be more specific. Client confidentiality."

She nodded, mulling that over.

"You don't look like you approve."

She tried to smooth out her features. "That would make a good cover if you didn't want people to know what you were really doing."

He laughed. "Yeah. I guess it would."

She didn't join him in the laugh. After several seconds, he set down his mug. "So what kind of papers do you pick up and deliver early in the morning?"

"I'm an accountant. I keep financial records for various clients."

"Like who?"

"Oh, that's confidential," she answered, dredging up a laugh of her own. The laugh died and her mouth went dry as she caught a flicker of movement in the street outside the window.

"It's him," she gasped.

Chapter Three

Sara saw Alex swivel around to follow her gaze and zero in on the green truck driving down the street, now at a moderate pace. He was out of his seat before she could take a breath. And out the door before she could blink. She pushed back her own chair and stood up, leaning toward the window as she watched the chase.

Unfortunately, the driver of the pickup must have been alert for trouble, because she saw him step on the gas when Alex hit the sidewalk. Alex ran down the block after the vehicle, and she had to concede that the man was definitely a runner. His stride was long, his form graceful. But even an Olympic champion couldn't keep up with an internal combustion engine. She saw the truck put on a burst of speed, laying down a cloud of exhaust fumes as it disappeared.

When Alex came running back down the sidewalk, his hands were clenched at his sides.

His first word when he reached their table was a curse. Then an apology. "Sorry."

"I think you gave it your best shot," she murmured, her chest tight.

He settled back into his seat, breathing a little hard but not puffing the way she would have been after a chase like that. Well, not quite like that. In her high-heel shoes, she wouldn't have gotten half a block.

"The license plate was smeared with mud. But some of it had flaked off. I got part of the number. Maybe I can—" He stopped suddenly.

"Maybe you can what?"

He sighed. "Figure out the ownership from the DMV database."

She considered that for a moment. "How do you have access to that?"

"Through my company."

"I thought only police officers could do that."

"This isn't a subject that we should be discussing," he said.

She leaned back in her chair and studied him. "That's a convenient excuse. What else are you not telling me?"

She had the satisfaction of seeing a quick, evasive look in his eyes. Then he shrugged and asked, "What makes you think I'm not?"

She gave him her own shrug. "Nothing I can put my finger on."

"Good. Because I want to ask you something. Whose toes have you stepped on lately?"

"Nobody's."

"Are you sure?"

"What are you getting at?"

"When I pulled you out of the way of that truck, it looked like it was heading straight for you. I mean deliberately."

She felt the blood drain out of her face. "No!"

"It's like he was waiting around the corner for you to step off the curb. As soon as you did, he came barreling onto Main Street."

"Is that the opinion of a professional security expert?"

"Yes. So you'd better think about who might be out to get you."

"Nobody!"

"Maybe it's connected to one of your clients. Who do you work for?"

"I'm certainly not going to tell you. Did you ask me to have a cup of coffee so you could interrogate me, or are you trying to scare me?"

"I'm trying to make sure you take care of yourself."

"Why should you care?"

"I like you."

She made a snorting sound. "How could you? You don't know me."

The words hung in the air between them. Lord, *did* he remember? Was he playing the same game as she—pretending they were strangers?

"I make quick judgments about people," he finally said.

"So do I. And I don't trust you."

"You don't think we connected a little while ago?"

No! She wouldn't let that be true.

She stood, aware that Blake was watching them from the other side of the room and thinking that half of St. Stephens would know about this conversation by the end of the day. Lowering her voice, she said, "You're making me uncomfortable. There's something you're not telling me, and I don't like deceit."

"Oh, don't you?"

"What's that supposed to mean?"

"Forget it."

"Right. I will." Turning, she whirled away from him and marched out of the coffee shop, sure that she had made a mistake by not fleeing Alex Shane the moment she'd realized who he was.

As soon as she hit the sidewalk, she started to shake.

Somehow she'd controlled herself in his presence, sat there across from him as if her insides weren't churning. Now that she was alone, she stumbled down the block toward her car. Once she was inside, she ground the engine, then almost turned into the path of a car coming too fast through the business district.

"Get a grip," she muttered, although some part of her silently acknowledged that she had a right to be shaken. Two bad things had happened this morning: Someone had almost run her over, then a man she'd never expected to see again had held her in his arms, and she'd reacted to him the way she had all those years ago. Back then she'd known he was dangerous. Maybe he was even more dangerous now.

Luckily, her house was close to the historic downtown district, because she wasn't sure how far she could have driven in her present condition. She unlocked the back door, sprinted through the kitchen and collapsed into one of the overstuffed chairs that she'd bought at an auction a few years ago.

Alex Shane!

Part of her had been relieved when she'd heard he'd left the area. Because there was no place in her life for the wanton, out-of-control girl she'd been that night at the State Park.

A group of her friends had heard about where the interesting kids from St. Stephens High hung out. Had heard about their fun parties. She'd been nervous about going along, but she hadn't wanted to look like a chicken so she'd agreed. Besides, she hated the way Mom and Dad were always on her, restricting her, making sure she was a good little girl. That was why they'd sent her to Catholic school, when she wasn't even Catholic.

At first she'd stuck close to her friends. But after a few

beers, she was feeling braver. And when she saw this drop-dead gorgeous guy eyeing her, she'd wondered what it would be like to kiss him.

They were in a public park, she reasoned. Nothing major could happen. And when her friends started urging her to go on up and talk to him, she boldly sauntered across the clearing that separated them.

His eyes swept up and down her body in a way that sent tingles of fear and arousal over her skin. "What's a sheltered little girl like you doing here?" he asked.

"I came to meet you," she answered brashly. "What's your name?"

"Alex. How about you?"

"Sara."

There was some back-and-forth conversation—witty on his part, with her working hard to keep up. He moved closer, draped his arm around her shoulder, his fingers playing with her upper arm, sending currents of sensation through her.

She'd made out with boys before. Clumsy boys whose kisses were a whole lot less potent than the light touch of Alex's fingers on her arm.

Then he murmured, "I like you a lot... You want to go somewhere private with me so we can get to know each other better?"

Her brain was still functioning enough for her to feel a little zing of alarm. "I can't go off with you. I've got to stay here with my friends."

"Well, we don't have to go very far. We can just sit in the back seat of my car."

"I—"

"Come on. We won't do anything you don't want to do. I promise."

Somewhere in her mind she knew that she shouldn't

trust him, but he made everything seem all right. With his words and his gestures and the warm look in his eyes.

She gave him a little nod, let him link his fingers with hers and lead her to one of the cars parked in the darkness under the pine trees.

It started slowly, with light kisses, the gentle stroking of his hands through her hair, across her back.

It scared her when he cupped her breasts. Scared her because it felt too good. She prided herself on keeping control with boys. But she'd never felt this way before. Like her skin was suddenly too tight. Like intimate parts of her were hot and tingling and begging for his touch.

He didn't push her. He backed off when she insisted he stop, soothed her with little kisses and reassuring words so that she didn't do the smart thing and get out of the car.

Instead, she let him touch her again in that thrilling, arousing way of his. She felt her breasts aching for his touch, felt her nipples contract to tight points, heard her own breath coming fast and urgent.

She didn't stop him this time when he went even further—slipping his hand under her T-shirt, unhooking her bra. And when he brought his hands around to cup her breasts, stroke his thumbs over the tight crests, she moaned into his mouth.

Rolling up her shirt, he found one distended nipple with his mouth, circled it with his tongue, then sucked on it, sending a bolt of sensation surging downward through her body.

He kept up the delicious torture, increasing her pleasure as he took the other nipple between his thumb and finger, squeezing and tugging and twisting, so that there was no room in her brain for thoughts—only needs and sensations she had never imagined before.

She had forgotten where she was. Forgotten her friends.

Forgotten everything but Alex and what he was doing to her. And when he lifted her onto his lap and pressed the hot, aching part of her against himself, she was helpless to do anything besides rock against him and seek more of the wonderful torture he was inflicting on her.

A distant jangling sound pulled her out of the memory. It took several seconds for her to figure out that the phone was ringing.

She stood quickly, swaying on her feet, then dashed across the room and picked up the receiver.

"Hello?"

There was no answer.

"Hello?"

She could hear breathing on the other end of the line, feel a prickle of apprehension at the back of her neck.

"Who's there?"

The connection snapped off and she was left listening to static. Slowly she replaced the phone in its cradle, then she went down the hall to her office and looked at the caller ID. It said "Pay Phone."

Great. No help.

Probably a wrong number, she told herself, although if that were true, why had the person on the other end of the line hung on so long?

Uneasy, her mind backed away from the phone call, and landed back on the previous topic.

She'd been deep into memories of Alex Shane. She hadn't known his last name when she'd been in the car with him, but one of her friends had told her on the way home.

She'd been angry with him for tempting her so far and angry with herself for letting it happen. Making out had never gotten to her the way it had gotten to her with Alex. She'd always been slightly detached, always slightly amused at the way guys got hot and bothered. And she'd always stopped them before they ever went too far. With Alex, she'd been completely caught up in the experience. He'd been the one in control.

She shivered. What if he had progressed to taking off her shorts? Would she have had the presence of mind to stop him, or would she have let him have intercourse with her?

Probably. Because she'd been too naive to fully understand what was happening. But he'd let her off easy. She'd been thankful, and at the same time angry. Angry with herself and angry with him for being so good at pleasing a woman. If she'd come away from the experience with anything, it was the determination never to let it happen again.

It had been a long time before she'd let herself get into a similar situation. She laughed. Not similar, exactly. Nothing she'd experienced had ever been similar. She'd never again let herself be pushed into anything she couldn't handle.

Over the years, she'd learned how to enjoy herself, but she hadn't allowed herself to lose perspective. Hadn't let herself slip into that wild, abandoned place where she was totally vulnerable.

She'd been too wary for that. She was still too wary, and she didn't like coming face-to-face with the man who had been so instrumental in shaping her behavior.

Probably she should thank him, she thought with a little snort. He'd helped her focus her life, understand the importance of staying in control.

Which she was now, she told herself. She wasn't going to let Alex Shane change that. She wasn't going to let herself get spooked by the wrong number or the incident with the truck, or any of the other things that had happened lately. Things she didn't want to think about too much.

She was going to get to work on the papers Lee Tillman had asked her to pick up.

ALEX SAT in front of his dark computer, restless and angry with himself.

He'd screwed things up with Sara Delaney. She was a suspect, and it didn't matter whether he remembered hot sex with her or not. He should never have gotten himself into a situation where he had to answer questions that were inconvenient.

But his lack of finesse with Sara was only a secondary problem. His primary concern was the disappearance of Lee Tillman. Maybe talking to the chief of police wouldn't be such a bad idea.

He'd seen Clark Hempstead around town, and the man hadn't changed much. In his mind, he pictured the police chief sitting behind his battered metal desk, his chair tipped back at a dangerous angle, his belly protruding above a pair of blue uniform pants worn comfortably low. Strands of dark hair would be combed across his balding skull. His metal-framed glasses, which he'd had for so long that they were coming back into style, would be slid halfway down his nose. And there might be a bit of sugar from a doughnut on his upper lip.

Eleven years ago, Alex had hated the man's guts. Now he understood that Hempstead was good for St. Stephens.

Like Alex, the chief had left the Eastern Shore to attend school at the University of Maryland, College Park. Only Hempstead had come back right after graduation to serve the people of his community.

Once, Alex had sneered at the man's small-town values. Now he understood him better. Understood that he had dedicated himself to the community where he'd grown up, which was more than Alex could say for himself.

The sergeant who answered the phone put him through right away.

"Hempstead speaking," the eerily familiar voice said.

"This is Alex Shane."

"Heard you were in town."

"Yes. I'm on an assignment for Randolph Security," he answered, feeling as if he had to establish his legitimacy right away.

"They're a well-respected outfit. But weren't you with the Howard County P.D. before you joined Randolph?"

"News gets around."

"You're one of St. Stephens' success stories."

Alex shifted in his seat, glad that the chief couldn't see his face. "A living legend, hmm?" he muttered.

"You turned yourself around real well, son. From juvie to cop. That's notable."

"Well, you put the fear of God into me," Alex heard himself saying.

Hempstead laughed, then cut to the chase. "Did you call to hash over old battle scars? Or do we have some present business?"

"I don't know. I'm calling to lay out a situation, see what you think."

"I'm at your service."

"Since you seem to have a handle on everything that goes on in town, you probably know Lee Tillman has Randolph Security on retainer. Tillman called me this morning at the crack of dawn. He was upset and insisted that he needed to see me right away. He said he'd leave the front door unlocked. I went in, but the house was empty. He'd told me he was leaving on a trip, and there was a notation on his calendar to that effect. There was no real sign of foul play, but the expensive oriental rug in his office was missing. I couldn't help thinking that it would make a wonderful wrapper for a body.''

"You think something's happened to him? That he didn't just leave town on his own?''

"I'm going to talk to his girlfriend, Dana Eustice. See if she knows where he went.''

"Did Tillman tell you what he wanted when he called?''

"He wasn't willing to discuss it over the phone. But I got the feeling he thought he was in danger.''

"From anything he said?'' Hempstead probed.

"Nothing concrete. Just what I picked up from the tone of his voice.''

Alex pictured the chief rubbing his finger against his lips as he mulled that over for several seconds. ''Yeah, I know what you mean. Still, that's not much to go on. And it's too soon to file a missing person's report. What do you want from me?''

"I just want you to be aware of the situation in case you hear anything.''

"If I do, I'll put you in the loop.'' The chief hesitated for a moment, then cleared his throat. ''Do you want me to have a talk with Ms. Eustice and see what she knows?''

Alex was glad Hempstead couldn't see the look of surprise on his face. ''Wouldn't that be unusual at this stage?''

The man on the other end of the line laughed. ''Son, this is a small town, not the big city. I recall that Ms. Eustice stops in at the Decoy on Thursdays for lunch with some of the people in her theater group. They're discussing what production to put on next.''

"Something where she's the star,'' Alex murmured, remembering that Dana Eustice liked to be the center of attention. Since Lee Tillman was one of the main backers of the theater company, his girlfriend was likely to get what she wanted.

"I can pick up a sandwich there and ask how Lee's doing," the chief was saying.

"I appreciate that."

"I'll let you know how it goes."

Alex hung up feeling that Chief Hempstead was willing to go the extra mile for him—an odd sensation given their previous history.

For several moments, he sat staring into space. Then he rolled toward his desk and booted up his computer. First he searched Motor Vehicles for the license number from this morning. But he didn't have enough letters and numbers to net him anything.

With a sigh, he connected to the very comprehensive and very expensive information service that Randolph Security used and typed in Sara Delaney's name.

Someone had tried to run her down that morning. He was sure of it. Of course, he'd never thought that a hit-and-run was the best way to get rid of an enemy. It had the advantage of looking like an accident, but it was pretty uncertain. After all, you might not kill the victim and then you'd be left with unfinished business.

The thought sent a trickle of cold through him. He hadn't been kidding Sara. She was in some kind of trouble, whether she knew it or not, and maybe he could find out what it was.

The first thing he discovered was that the E was for Ellen. In less than an hour he discovered that Sara Ellen Delaney had been born in St. Stephens twenty-eight years ago. Her parents were Reid and Brenda Delaney, who had started buying savings bonds for their daughter the year she was born, and had obtained a social security number for her at the same time. Brenda Delaney had died a couple of years ago of a heart attack at age sixty. Reid, aged sixty-five, still lived in the house where Sara had grown up. Although Reid had worked as a machinist at White and Sandler Tools, a local manufacturing plant, he and his wife had managed to send their daughter to the University of Maryland, Baltimore County, without taking out any loans for tuition.

Sara had majored in accounting, and her grades had been mostly As and Bs, with a C in biology. She'd gotten three campus traffic tickets, which she'd paid promptly. She'd begun preparing tax returns to earn money before she graduated, and she'd passed the CPA exam on her first try. One of her earliest clients had been Lee Tillman, who'd hired her in her junior year.

Indeed, Sara appeared to be doing awfully well for someone still in her late-twenties. She had made a down payment on her house and was paying off the mortgage at seven percent—a very favorable interest rate. She ran her accounting business from an office on the second floor of her home. She had no dependents, but she gave her father two hundred dollars a month.

Her car was paid for, and unlike many women, she took it in for regular maintenance. Currently she had a clean driving record, except for a citation, issued by one of Hempstead's deputies, for failing to brake at a stop sign at the end of her street. Her two credit card balances ran between five hundred and a thousand a month each, which she paid off before accruing interest. Finally, she seemed to be in good health, and the only prescription medication she'd taken in the past five years was Keflex, when she'd had a case of bronchitis in February.

Alex leaned back in his desk chair and clasped his hands behind his head. Every time he did a Strategic Stats search, he got a little paranoid, thinking about somebody doing the same thing on him. It was downright frightening how much he had learned about Ms. Sara Ellen Delaney without her knowledge, and he couldn't help feeling a little twinge of conscience. Assuming, of course, that she was innocent of any wrongdoing.

She'd seemed innocent enough when he'd sat across from her in the coffee shop this morning. Well, perhaps she'd been a little wary. But he could account for that by his own behavior. He'd been evasive when she'd asked him questions, and she'd bristled.

But her innocence and her reaction to his nonanswers could both be calculated to create an effect. Looks could be deceiving. He'd once been fooled by a seventy-year-old grandmother who'd seemed nice as pie. Then he'd discovered she'd poisoned three husbands to get their insurance money.

He hadn't been turned on by the grandmother, of course. Unfortunately, despite his wish for personal detachment, he had been turned on by Sara Delaney. This morning she'd brought out his protective instincts, as well.

He didn't trust either response, nor did he trust his judgment when it came to women. He'd thought Cindy loved him, and he'd been dead wrong.

And he was damned if he was going to repeat the mistake by letting Sara Delaney take him in. It didn't matter what had happened eleven years ago between himself and Ms. Delaney. That had no relevance today.

So until evidence to the contrary, he was going to assume that she was up to no good, even though he'd discovered nothing overtly criminal. There still was the question of how she'd gotten so successful so quickly.

Leaning forward again, he clicked the mouse. A couple of seconds later, the printer started spitting out the details of Ms. Delaney's life. Old habits died hard, he thought as he got out a file folder and shoved the papers inside. Some people would have been content with the information tucked away on a hard drive. He liked a real folder with sheets of paper he could read in bed if he felt like it.

After tossing the file onto his desk, he got up and stretched, then made another pot of coffee and poured himself a mug.

Sipping from it, he came back to the computer to run another background check. He typed in the name of the man who had called him this morning sounding frightened—then hadn't shown up for their appointment. At first, he found no surprises. Lee Tillman owned The Refuge free and clear. He also owned his Lexus and his Jag. His credit card bills were much steeper than Ms. Delaney's, yet he always paid them at the end of the period. He belonged to the Optimists, the Jaycees, the First Methodist Church and the Society of Wine Connoisseurs. He had several pending parking tickets, and several points on his license—enough that if he got another moving violation, he was in danger of having his license suspended. His birthday was May 9, 1947, and he'd been born in New York City.

However, no record existed that stated where Lee had gone to school, nor did it seem he'd ever visited a doctor or dentist. There was no information on his parents or any other relatives. He had never held a job. He had no previous addresses, nor had he paid a utility, tax or telephone bill before moving to St. Stephens, Maryland. His driver's license had been issued twenty-seven years ago and so had his social security card—unusual in a day and age when every bank account required a social security number for tax purposes.

Alex tried every database in the system but they all drew the same blank. Rocking back in his chair, he rubbed his eyes, wondering if anybody else ever had tried to dig up information on Lee Tillman before. If they had, he was certain they would have discovered what he was discovering: For all intents and purposes, the man had sprung into existence twenty-seven years ago, when he'd appeared in St. Stephens, Maryland, bought his estate and deposited large sums of money at several local banks.

From the shadows of the computer screen, Lee seemed to give him a sardonic wink. Alex's expression was stony as he stared back. He'd started this investigation because he'd felt both a personal and a professional obligation to Lee. Now that he knew the man had gone to a great deal of trouble to bury almost half the years of his life, he felt suckered. What the hell was Lee trying to hide—that he'd beamed down to earth from the *Starship Enterprise?*

Alex felt the hair on the back of his neck tingle as an only slightly less preposterous hypothesis struck him. The Master of the Refuge might have sprung to life from the shadows of some previous existence and now had vanished back into those shadows. What if he wasn't dead at all? What if he'd simply arranged to *disappear* from St. Stephens as efficiently and as mysteriously as he had appeared all those years ago?

Chapter Four

Propping an elbow on the desk and his chin on his hand, Alex stared at the monitor as his mind played with the bizarre theory. What if Lee had been laying the groundwork for this all month, ever since he'd asked Randolph Security to investigate his associates. He'd let Alex Shane poke around in his private life. Then he'd awakened him with an urgent early-morning phone call.

He'd known Alex would come running, and find the house empty and the rug missing.

Eyes narrowed, Alex considered the idea. If you were going to fake a murder, wouldn't you leave more evidence around? Signs of a struggle…blood? Well, maybe not—if you wanted things to be ambiguous.

He shook his head. The whole scenario was a huge stretch. But it wasn't impossible. He'd always known that Lee Tillman was tricky and devious. He hadn't known just how far the man was capable of going—until he'd started digging into his past.

So was Sara Delaney part of the plot? Had Lee arranged for her to be in the house because he knew that Alex would probably be there? Or had someone else come in and killed Lee Tillman, or kidnapped him? Or maybe this wasn't about murder. Maybe it was about blackmail. Because if

Alex had dug into Lee's background, maybe someone else had done the same thing, and threatened to reveal that Lee had a false identity unless the man came across with a huge sum. Unwilling to pay the tariff, Lee had chosen to disappear as effectively as he'd appeared.

With a sigh, Alex dug the phone book out of the desk drawer and started calling companies that cleaned oriental rugs. Posing as a befuddled home owner who couldn't remember where he'd sent his precious oriental, Alex asked if each establishment had picked up a rug from Lee Tillman. Nobody had. Which didn't prove anything. For all Alex knew, Lee could have taken the rug with him in the car and dropped it off on the Western Shore on his way north.

There wasn't much more Alex was going to find out sitting home. So he left the house again and headed toward a ramshackle collection of homes strung out along Crisfield Creek. He'd been here before, long ago. Now he felt his chest tighten as he climbed out of the car and walked down toward the water where a man in a torn T-shirt and faded jeans was leaning into the open hood of an old Ford.

"Lewis Farmer?"

The man straightened and stared at him, his eyes widening as he realized who it was. More than once, he and Alex had beaten the crap out of each other. Alex had been the leader of his pack. Lewis had wanted to prove he was just as tough.

"Alex Shane," he said, his voice milder than Alex might have expected. Reaching for a rag that lay on one fender of the car, he wiped his grimy hands. "What brings you down to the St. Stephens slums?"

"I wouldn't call it the slums."

"Yeah, well, we can skip the niceties. What do you want?"

"I'm looking for Lee Tillman."

"He doesn't apprise me of his social plans."

"You work for him. When's the last time you saw him?"

"Last week." Farmer's gaze turned inward. "Tuesday, I guess. He wanted me to haul some more rocks down to the riverbank."

"And you took care of that?"

"Yeah. I took care of it. He pays good."

"And you don't know where he might be now."

"Said he was going on vacation. Said he wanted the shoreline reinforced so the house wouldn't wash away while he was gone."

Alex nodded. That sounded like Lee, all right. Pulling out a business card, he extended it to Farmer.

The other man took it in his grimy hand. "Fancy! What's Randolph Security?"

"It's a combination security company and detective agency," he answered, thinking that it was also a whole lot more. But he didn't need to spell out the particulars. "Give a call if you see Lee. I'm paying cash for information."

"You don't have to bribe me, Alex."

"I'd appreciate the help."

Farmer gave him a smile that didn't meet his eyes. "Sure thing."

Alex turned and left, almost positive that Lewis Farmer wasn't going to give him any information—even if he had it.

Alex pondered Farmer's involvement. Had someone paid him to help get rid of Lee? Or did he have a motive for doing it on his own?

Back in his car, Alex headed for the business district of

St. Stephens. His first stop was the real estate office of Emmett Bandy.

It was ironic, he thought, that residents from across the bay were scarfing up property on the shore when many of the people who had lived here for years couldn't afford to keep their homes. With the closing down of some local businesses and the dying off of the seafood industry, properties that had once been owned by honest working people were being torn down and replaced by expensive residences.

Emmett Bandy was part of the process. His business was good, but he'd made the mistake of believing his own publicity. He'd seen a speculative opportunity in the housing market and had borrowed fifty thousand dollars for a down payment from Lee Tillman. Then the heirs of the man who had sold him the property had disputed the sale, and Emmett had been left in the lurch. Lee hadn't let their friendship stop him from demanding repayment and there had been harsh words exchanged.

Alex had planned to spend twenty minutes in the real estate office, looking at pictures of selected properties, pretending that he wanted to change his status from renter to home owner before bringing up the subject of Lee Tillman. But it took only five seconds to ascertain that Emmett wasn't in a position to have murdered Tillman and disposed of the body. His arm was in a sling—broken and dislocated from a fall down some unstable steps at a property he'd been showing a few days earlier. So unless he'd had help, he wasn't the one who had frightened Lee so badly that morning.

Alex's next stop was the drugstore at the corner of Main and Duke Streets. The establishment was a holdover from the days when there had been fewer shops in town, many doing double or triple duty. So in addition to the pharmacy in the back and the variety of dry goods stocked in front, there was also a coffee shop where many of the locals hung out. Outsiders were barely tolerated at the scarred Formica-topped tables.

But many of the regulars remembered Alex from his younger days. So while he drank another cup of coffee, he shot the breeze with retired watermen and housewives who had known his mother. They had varying disparaging comments to make about Lee Tillman—comments that would have been imprudent on the part of a murderer. Although they might have been designed to throw up a smoke screen, Alex conceded. And he got little dividend from the conversation.

Pete Williams, who was retired from the fire department, made a point of mentioning that Alex's only sibling, Billy, had gotten into some trouble last night at the Cat Walk, a local bar where he and his lowlife friends hung out.

Unlike Alex, Billy hadn't escaped their shared past. He'd progressed from juvenile crime to adult offenses, which had led to several short stretches in the county jail and then the federal penitentiary at Jessup. Now he was out of the joint and back in town, where he apparently couldn't stay out of trouble, although Alex only knew about his brother's problems secondhand, since they hadn't spoken in years.

He could have sought Billy out, he supposed. But he knew from past experience that would only have led to a confrontation. The kid would never put it in these terms, but Alex knew Billy was resentful that his brother had escaped their heritage. Alex had figured out during the year after high school that there was no future for him on the shore and he'd turned his life around. Billy had stayed and dug himself into a hole that was too big to climb out of.

Alex hung out at the coffee shop for over an hour, turning the talk back to that eccentric Lee Tillman, hearing various comments about the man. But Alex was pretty sure he wasn't talking to anyone who'd done the man in that morning.

He was still mulling over suspects when he stepped out onto the street and spotted a short, slender woman coming out of the In Style Beauty Salon.

It was Dana Eustice, Lee Tillman's girlfriend. Her blond hair had just been curled into a soft pageboy that flattered her longish face. And as always, she was impeccably turned out, this afternoon in a rose-colored tunic dress.

She was in her mid-fifties. But she was one of those women who fought tooth and nail to keep herself looking young, probably with the help of a plastic surgeon, Alex judged as he studied her taut jawline.

His car was in the same parking lot, so it was no problem to meet up with her as she stopped beside a beige Lincoln Town Car.

"Dana."

She raised her head slowly. "Why, it's Alex Shane, isn't it?"

"That's right."

He studied her open expression, thinking that she looked as though she had nothing in the world to hide.

"I had an appointment with Lee this morning, but he stood me up. You don't happen to know where he is, do you?"

She tilted her blond head to one side. "You're the second person who's asked me about him today. He was heading for Nova Scotia. Cape Breton Island. He wanted to get away to a place where he could relax."

"So you know where he's staying?"

"The Inverary Inn, but since he's driving, he won't be there for five or six days."

"Okay. Thanks. If you talk to him, tell him I'm concerned."

"Yes."

He watched her get into her car, thinking that if she was worried about Lee, she was doing a darn good job of hiding that fact.

After she'd pulled away, he got into his SUV and drove to the Crab Claw, the rambling old restaurant on the town dock.

"I can give you a table in fifteen or twenty minutes," the cute little hostess told him. "But you can sit in the bar."

"Thanks."

He ordered a beer and listened in on more town gossip as he sat by the window, gazing out over the water, watching some of the swans who made their home in the marsh along one side of the town's harbor.

He'd been up since before dawn, and after a meal of crab cakes and french fries, he thought about calling it a day. Instead, he found himself heading back toward Redbud Street. It was getting dark, and several lights were on in Sara's house. He drove slowly by, circled the block, then pulled up under a maple tree across the street. Cutting the engine, he slumped down in his seat and turned his gaze toward the house. He felt his heartbeat quicken as he saw Sara step in front of a window. She seemed to be looking out into the night as if she sensed someone was watching her.

It made him feel guilty again—guilty about spying on her. But that didn't stop him from taking her in. In the soft light from the room, her hair had a golden glow. She'd changed from her business suit and blouse into a T-shirt and sweatpants that hugged her curves. The outfit made her look like the teenager he remembered, not the twenty-eight-year-old woman he knew she was. His chest tightened as he thought of that long-ago night.

It was difficult to believe that she had anything to do with Lee Tillman's disappearance—or anything to do with Lee Tillman, for that matter. But he'd seen her walk into the man's office as if she owned the place. Not only that, he had a gut feeling that she was a key piece in the puzzle he was trying to put together, and he'd learned not to ignore his hunches.

So what was he expecting exactly? That she was working with an accomplice, and he'd show up at her house while the man from Randolph Security was watching? Maybe it was Lewis Farmer. Maybe the two of them had murdered Lee Tillman and gotten rid of the body.

He snorted softly in the darkness. Yet it wasn't out of the question that she was expecting company—and the meeting was related to her visit to The Refuge this morning.

He made himself comfortable in the SUV. It had been a long, frustrating day, and he fought a dragging feeling of fatigue. Idly he wondered how Ms. Delaney would react if he climbed out of the 4Runner, crossed the street and knocked on the door. Probably sprint straight to the phone and call Chief Hempstead.

And what would he do if he knocked on the door? Tell her he was sorry about the way things had ended this afternoon. Remind her they'd had a great time together eleven years ago. Then tell her she was the first woman in months he'd wanted to take to bed. Right! That would certainly be smart.

Still, as he stared at her, he contemplated how her pretty little mouth had tasted under his—and how it would taste now. And how her rounded breasts had felt in his hands. He tried to abort those thoughts when he felt himself getting carried away. But suddenly the long months of celibacy were making blood pool in the lower part of his body.

He was still sitting there, still mulling over his conflicted emotions, when a vehicle came slowly down the quiet street. It was a pickup, but a different make and model than the one that tried to run Sara down. Older than the previous vehicle. In the dark he couldn't see the color, and there was no light illuminating the license plate.

Alex watched it drift down the block, then breathed out a little sigh as it rolled on past. Surely he wasn't going to get jumpy every time he saw a pickup.

His heart had resumed its normal pace, when the vehicle came into view again. This time it pulled to the curb several houses down from Sara's place. Seconds after the lights winked out, a man stepped onto the street and looked up and down the block.

In the darkness Alex thought it really was Lewis Farmer. Then he saw the man's hair was shorter than Farmer's, and his shoulders were too wide. It was some other lowlife type—somebody he didn't recognize.

Alex slid lower in his seat, his breath shallow as he waited to find out if he'd been spotted. Apparently the darkness hid him.

The guy from the truck walked rapidly up the sidewalk, still looking around furtively. When he reached Sara's property, he stepped off the sidewalk and onto the driveway. Then he disappeared from view as he rounded the side of the house.

Alex was out of his SUV moments later, torn by the need for caution and the need to find out exactly what was going on: A meeting or a clandestine attack?

He moved quickly and quietly across the street, then used the car in the driveway for cover as he made his way cautiously toward the house. He saw only a few lights on and wondered if Sara was expecting the guy.

He hated the direction of his thoughts, yet he couldn't dismiss them.

The man had disappeared. Alex stopped to check the side door, but it was locked, which proved nothing. Instinct led him to look for another way into the house. As he turned the corner, he encountered an open door.

His first impulse was to bolt inside, but his police training had taught him caution. Gliding up to the door, he strained his ears and heard a man speaking.

"Nice and easy, honey."

"What do you want?" Her voice was high and reedy.

Alex clenched his hands in frustration. He still couldn't tell what was going on—not just from hearing those two lines. All he knew was that Sara was in trouble. His heart was pounding like a jackhammer as he forced himself to wait and find out more.

The man was speaking again, answering her question. "I think you know."

"Please, don't hurt me."

There was a pause before the man answered, "Now that depends on how well you cooperate."

"What do you want? Money?"

"That's a good start."

"I don't have much in my purse."

"What about upstairs, in your bedroom drawer?"

"Yes. Okay."

Damn! Alex cursed himself for not having a weapon with him. As a police detective, he'd always carried a gun, even when he was off duty. But Randolph operatives didn't walk around armed unless there was a reason to carry. There was a reason now, but his Sig was back in his rented house.

"Get going," the man inside said.

Alex wondered what kind of weapon he had? No matter, the guy wasn't planning to kill her immediately. If he was planning to kill her at all.

Still, Alex knew that he was making assumptions that were tantamount to gambling with Sara Delaney's life.

The voices moved off, toward the stairs, he presumed. Alex waited half a minute, then as silently as possible he stepped into the house, his eyes scanning the scene. There was nothing out of place, nothing to indicate that an assailant had come in and threatened the occupant. Yet the rank smell of sweat hung in the air. Sweat from a man who hadn't bathed in a couple of days.

Alex crossed the room and made for the stairs.

Sara's voice drifted down, high-pitched and frightened. His heart leaped into his throat as he pounded toward the stairs.

A crash reverberated from the floor above then a snarling curse. Alex took the stairs two at a time, found Sara, and the man struggling in the upper hall.

If the guy had a gun, he wasn't using it, Alex thought as he flung himself onto the attacker's back, wrenching him away from Sara.

She gave a strangled cry, but Alex was only peripherally aware of her. His attention was focused on the man, who growled another curse as he whirled around, his fist raised. Alex ducked the blow, then sent his own fist into a hard jaw. It was too dark in the hallway to see much of the assailant's face but a fleeting impression of sallow cheeks and fierce eyes. Then he was too busy fighting for his life.

The guy knew what he was doing. He went for the throat and Alex felt his breath choking off, saw black spots dancing behind his eyes and coalescing into an overwhelming void. Knowing he had only seconds to react, he brought his elbows up in a swift, sharp move, connecting with the guy's arms. The hold around his neck loosened just enough for him to draw in a breath. Then he heard a flurry of movement, heard a hard object connecting with flesh and bone. In the next second, the guy's hands fell away.

Alex crashed back against the wall, gasping for breath as he watched the assailant slide to the floor. Sara was standing behind him, a lamp clasped in her hands.

Then her eyes focused on Alex, and she gasped. "You."

"Yeah."

"What are you doing here?"

"I—"

The attacker moaned. Then before either one of them could move, he was reaching for his boot. Metal gleamed in his hand. A knife blade.

Alex was already dodging aside when the knife flew through the air. It would have hit him in the chest if he'd been where he'd been standing seconds earlier. Instead, it skimmed the fleshy part of his arm and he felt a hot slice of pain. He heard the knife clatter to the floor. When he looked up again, the man was in motion, diving for one of the doors in the hallway.

Alex flung himself after the fleeing figure, knowing his reaction time was slowed by the pain in his arm and the still-muzzy feeling in his head. Before he could dodge aside again, the guy turned and kicked him in the chest. Alex went flying backward as the other man flung himself toward a window.

The man yanked up the sash and dived through, onto the roof of the first-floor porch. Alex plunged after him, but the assailant was already across the roof and swinging his leg over the side. By the time Alex reached the corner, the guy had hit the ground running and disappeared into the darkness.

Cursing, Alex limped back to the window, climbed inside and stood swaying on his feet. When he felt steady enough to move, he looked up, and saw Sara standing with her back against the wall, the lamp raised over her head.

"It's okay," he said wearily. "I'm not much of a threat."

The lamp wavered in her hand, but she didn't put it down.

"What are you doing here?" she demanded.

"Saving you from getting killed."

She made a low sound. "I brained him."

"Yeah," he answered, watching the lamp slide from her fingers and thunk to the rug.

In the moonlight slanting through the window, he could only dimly see the expression on her face, but he suspected she looked as dazed as he felt.

"What did the bastard do to you?" he demanded, taking a step toward her.

"Not too much," she answered on a sob.

He moved more swiftly then, closing the distance between them, reaching for her.

She didn't protest as he pulled her into his arms. In fact, she seemed to melt against him.

"Sara," he murmured, his voice rough as he folded her close, swamped by emotions he didn't want to examine too closely. He tried to concentrate on her, not his own reactions.

Fine tremors vibrated through her body.

"It's okay, sweetheart. You're all right," he soothed, unable to turn her loose. There was nothing wrong with comforting her until she was steady on her feet, he told himself. Then he'd let her go.

Somehow that goal faded to the back of his mind as his senses reacted on a dozen different levels. He felt her very feminine, fine-boned body, inhaled her familiar scent, like a fresh breeze blowing through his soul. At the same time, he was vividly conscious of the way her breasts pressed against his chest and her hands cupped his shoulders. He felt warmth spreading through him—physical warmth and something deeper.

"Alex," she sighed.

She raised her face to him, and his breath hitched. As he stared down into the depths of her eyes, he forgot the reason he'd taken her into his arms in the first place.

The intensity was too much. He felt it vibrating between them.

"Don't be afraid. I won't hurt you," he heard himself saying.

"I know," she whispered.

He was on sensory overload now. And at the same time, if he didn't have more of her, he would go mad. He gathered her closer, dizzy with the feel of her body against his.

Coherent thought fled his brain as he slanted his mouth over hers. She tasted as good as he remembered—of sweet innocence and of rich, dark promises.

As his mouth moved against hers, she made a small whimpering sound that only added to his out-of-control need. On a surge of desire, he increased the pressure of his lips on hers, urging her to open for him.

There was no resistance. She gave him what he wanted. Exactly what he wanted.

"Alex," she gasped into his mouth.

Needing no other invitation, he deepened the kiss.

Desire seemed to flow back and forth between them. He was rocking her against himself now, feasting on her mouth like a starving man invited to a banquet.

He felt as if he had come back to paradise as he explored the silky mass of her hair with one hand while the other drifted to her hips so that he could press the aching shaft of his erection more tightly against her.

"I'd forgotten anything could be this sweet," he groaned.

She didn't answer him in words, only angled her head to deepen the kiss, her own hands restless as they moved over his back and shoulders, then down his arms.

He heard her give a little gasp.

When she pulled away from him, he tried to draw her back.

But she shook her head, looking down in shock at her hand. It was covered with something dark and sticky.

Blood. His blood.

Chapter Five

Alex blinked as he stared at the blood, his gaze moving from her hand to his shirtsleeve. He was remembering suddenly that a knife had grazed his arm. Then Sara had captured his attention, and he'd forgotten all about getting cut.

"You need to go to the emergency room," she gasped out.

"It's just a flesh wound. If you have a towel, I can stop the bleeding."

"You need medical attention."

"Naw." He laughed. "I'm made of elephant hide."

Still, he was suddenly feeling unsteady on his feet. Maybe from the kiss. When she helped him into a chair, he didn't protest.

She snapped on the light, leaving him blinking as she disappeared from the room. She could be going to get a gun to finish him off, he thought, remembering why he'd been sitting outside her house in the first place.

His eyes zeroed in on her as she stepped back through the door, but she was only carrying a white towel. He was going to mess it up. Just the way he'd messed up her blouse, he noticed as he eyed the red splotch on her arm.

Avoiding her gaze, he rolled up his sleeve, then wrapped

the towel around his throbbing flesh, pressing at the line where blood oozed out.

The wound was superficial, but it was starting to hurt like a son of a bitch. Apparently, he'd been too busy earlier to focus on it.

When he looked up, Sara was staring at him.

"I didn't thank you," she said tightly.

He nodded. There were a dozen questions he wanted to ask her. Personal questions like what had she been feeling a few minutes ago in his arms and did she remember him. Instead, he stuck with, "Do you know that guy?"

"I never saw him before in my life."

"Okay."

"What's that supposed to mean?"

He gave a little shrug that ended with a wince, to his annoyance.

"You sound like you don't believe me."

He started to shrug again, then aborted the action. But he'd already made the mistake of letting her know he was in pain.

"Let me drive you to the hospital."

"Trying to get rid of me?"

She snorted. "I'm trying to get you medical attention, like I said."

They stared at each other, and he wanted to press the advantage, make her level with him, because he was sure she was hiding something. But he didn't have the energy for any kind of effective interrogation.

He was still trying to sort through what had happened between them a few minutes ago. He'd said something like, *I'd forgotten anything could be this sweet.* He hoped she didn't understand what he had meant: that he'd been remembering her, remembering them.

Perhaps she did remember all of it, too, and she was trying her damnedest to pretend it hadn't happened.

He tried to read her face, but she turned quickly away and disappeared again. When she returned, she was stepping briskly, carrying another towel, gauze, a basin of water, a cloth. Unwrapping the makeshift bandage, she kept her eyes away from his as she examined the wound. Blood was still oozing, although the flow had slowed.

He gritted his teeth, caught her regarding him, and made an effort at humor. "We have to stop meeting this way."

She answered with a little nod, not the laugh he'd hoped for.

"You need an antibiotic, I think," she said as she washed off the wound.

"Yeah. I've got some at home."

"Just like that—you've got the medicine you need?"

"My security company gave me an emergency medical kit," he replied laconically.

SARA WANTED TO press for answers. Actually, she suspected that she should demand answers, which she was pretty sure she wasn't going to get, judging from their last meeting.

When he'd failed to explain what he was doing in her house, she should have ordered him to leave. Yet he'd saved her—again—and she felt obligated to make sure he wasn't going to keel over on her account. Once she was satisfied he could leave under his own power, she'd kick him out.

And the sooner the better, because he was making her uneasy. Not just from the sudden flare of passion between them, although that was bad enough. If he'd gotten into her house so fast, he must have been right outside, watching her. Either that, or he'd followed the guy who had attacked her.

She poured antiseptic on the wound, knowing she was hurting him.

"When did you have your last tetanus shot?" she asked.

"Antibiotics. Antiseptic. Now tetanus shots. I thought you were an accountant not a doctor."

"I *am* an accountant. I'm just asking you one of the standard emergency-room questions."

"My tetanus vaccination is current."

Reaching for a couple of sterile gauze pads, she pressed them against the wound, watching his lips compress. "You're a macho bastard," she muttered.

"I've found that complaining doesn't do much good."

"I've found that cussing helps get you through the pain," she said as she secured the sterile pads with tape.

"I can't picture you cussing."

She laughed. "Then I hope you're not around when I hit my thumb with a hammer."

He joined her in the laughter, and she found she liked the sound of his chuckle. It was warm and deep—seductive, actually. She had to be careful. She found this man enormously appealing. Yet she still didn't know how he'd appeared on the scene at just the right time—twice.

"I think you'd better explain what you're doing here."

He leaned back in the chair, looking at her. She watched as he shifted his weight, stretching out his legs and crossing them at the ankles.

"Okay," he finally said, his gaze trained on her face. "Lee Tillman was worried that someone was trying to kill him. He hired my company, Randolph Security, to nose around St. Stephens. I've been down here since last month—investigating some of the people who have a beef against him."

"So what are you like—a hired gun in the Old West?"

"No. I'm not in the business of shooting until I've asked questions."

Was that supposed to be a joke? If so, it wasn't very funny, she thought as she struggled to keep her expression neutral.

Alex was speaking again. "Early this morning, he called me. He was panicked, wanted me to come over right away. So I pulled on some sweat clothes and drove to his estate. Following his orders, I parked in the woods down the road and came up along the river. I couldn't find Lee, so I searched the house. I was in his office when I heard the front door open and a woman coming up the stairs. I slipped into the closet so I could find out what she was up to."

Sara felt the hairs on the back of her neck bristle. She'd felt them stir when she was in Lee's office. Felt as if someone was watching her. Now she knew why. But she said nothing as she waited for him to finish his explanation.

"I saw her march in like she owned the place, go to a file cabinet and take out a folder. Then she left."

"You followed me into town! And you didn't say anything."

"As far as I'm concerned, you're a suspect."

The way he said it sent a shiver across her skin. "Suspected of what?"

"His murder for all I know."

"Murder! That's quite a stretch," she answered around the sudden knot in her throat. "He was supposed to be going on vacation."

"He was upset this morning when he called me. I believe he thought he was in danger. I have as much reason to think he was murdered as to think he's gone on a holiday. So do you want to tell me why you were at his place, in his office?''

"I don't owe you any explanations."

"We're going to get along a lot better if you level with me the way I just did with you."

She took a step back and folded her arms across her chest. "No we're not, because you're getting the hell out of my house."

"I don't think so."

"I'll call—" She stopped abruptly.

"The police?"

"Yes."

"Then why the hesitation?"

When she didn't answer, he continued, "Police Chief Hempstead already knows I'm working on the case. I didn't tell him I saw you at Lee's house this morning. He might be interested in knowing you were there."

She wondered if he was bluffing. She wondered about his motives. Still, she found herself on the defensive.

"I was picking up accounts he wanted me to work on." She blurted out what she hadn't intended to say.

He silently watched her for long moments, stroking his chin with his right hand, and she struggled not to squirm under his scrutiny. His gaze was penetrating, as if he could see through her skull, into her mind, and she hated the sensation.

"Can I see the papers?" he finally said.

"Certainly not! That's confidential information."

"Listen, I told you Lee Tillman has disappeared. If you want to help find him, you'll help me out. For example, did you notice anything strange about the office?"

"Like what?"

"Like something missing."

She had the kind of mind that paid attention to details.

That was how she'd become an accountant in the first place. Now, in her memory, she brought Lee's office into focus—the desk, the book shelves, the rug—

"The rug," she whispered. She hadn't been thinking about it that morning. Now she realized she hadn't felt it underfoot.

"So you noticed it, too. Well, that's a start."

"A start on what?"

"On the two of us cooperating."

"In your dreams."

His eyes narrowed. "You need my help and I'm willing to give it to you—in exchange for your coming clean with me."

"What do you mean by 'coming clean'?"

"You're hiding something."

She fought to keep herself from taking a step back. "I don't need anything from you."

"A pickup tried to run you down this morning. Then a man came in here and attacked you. Either he was someone you know or someone with reason to go after you, or both."

She kept her gaze steady. "For all I know, you sent the guy this morning. And then tonight, so you could rescue me and gain my confidence."

He gave a harsh laugh. "Oh, come on!"

"How do I know you were really in Lee's office?"

"I saw you go right to the file cabinet. After you took the folder out of the drawer, you stopped and adjusted your bra strap."

Her face heated at the memory.

"Then you took a peppermint candy from the dish on the table. You didn't put the wrapper in the trash, which made me wonder if you wanted to make sure nobody knew you'd been there."

"Bull! I had every right to be there. I have a key, in case you didn't notice." She glared at him. "You say you're with a security company. How do I know that's the truth?"

"You can call Cam Randolph, the head of the company, and ask if I work for him."

"Right. And he could be some guy you paid to make it look like you have a legitimate job."

He made an exasperated sound.

The air in the room seemed to vibrate with tension— and sexual awareness, which she did her best to ignore.

"I'm not guilty of anything!" she almost shouted.

"Prove it."

She folded her arms across her chest. "You mean like in a medieval witch-hunt. You dunk me in the water. If I float, I'm a witch. If I sink, I'm innocent."

"We could try it," he said dryly.

"We might as well, because you aren't going to believe anything I say."

He sighed. "Okay. If you have nothing to hide, what's your relationship with Lee Tillman?"

"I'm his accountant."

"That's all?"

"What are you suggesting, that I'm sleeping with him?"

"Are you?"

"Of course not. He's old enough to be my father," she almost shouted, thinking that protesting only made her seem more guilty in this man's eyes.

He was watching her with that unnerving keenness. "Old guys with lots of money turn on some women."

"Not me!" she retorted, hoping he wasn't going to ask what *did* turn her on.

"But you like him?"

That was a little easier to answer. She dragged in a

breath and let it out slowly, ordering herself to stay cool and calm. "He's gruff. He can be abrupt. But he's been pretty decent with me."

"Then help me find out what happened to him."

"Nothing happened," she answered, although she couldn't stop a small sliver of doubt from working its way into her mind. This morning she'd felt uneasy at Lee's house. But that was probably because Alex had been watching her.

Instead of giving her time to mull that over, he pressed on with more questions.

"You're sure he's just on vacation? Has he been the same recently, or has he struck you as being worried about something?"

She hunched her shoulders, considering. "He's been tense. But he doesn't confide in me. You say you're working for him. You should know more than I do."

"He hasn't been exactly straight with me either. Like you."

"How dare you."

Ignoring her quick flare of temper, he pushed himself out of the chair. "Okay, pack some clothing and your toilet articles."

"What?"

"Pack some things. You're coming home with me."

"I am not."

"Yes, you are. My gun's back home, and I can't protect you here."

"You think I'm going to go with you just like that?"

"Yeah, I do."

"And why is that?"

He gave her an impatient sigh. "Because you're in danger. And I think you're a smart woman. You're not going to sit around here waiting for someone to attack you again.

The guy could be outside in the bushes, watching for me to leave so he can come back and finish what he started.''

His words had the desired effect. Like a heroine in a classic horror movie, she felt a tremor go down her spine.

She knew from his face that he'd caught the reaction.

Quickly, he pressed his advantage. ''I'm not going to leave you in this house alone tonight. And I'm not staying here. We're going to my house. Don't worry, I'm not going to take you there and then tell you there's only one bed, and we have to share it.''

''You're damn right.''

''Let's stop wasting time. I need that antibiotic you mentioned earlier.''

She was damned if she did and damned if she didn't. If she went home with Alex Shane, then she was letting him call the shots—which was a dumb thing to do. On the other hand, staying here by herself was equally dumb. Alex could have scared her attacker off, but he was right: The assailant could be outside waiting to catch her alone again. Of course, the police were another option. But she had reasons for not calling them.

ALEX FOUND he was holding his breath, waiting for her decision. He needed to get home. Not to take an antibiotic but to use the special salve that Randolph had provided in the kit he'd brought with him. It would speed the healing process, and by tomorrow the wound would be no more than an annoyance.

But he wasn't going to tell that to Sara. And he wasn't going to let her stay here without protection.

Finally she sighed, then nodded. ''Okay.''

She disappeared from the room and was gone for several minutes. When she returned, she was carrying an overnight bag.

"I'll drive you," he said.

"More like I'll drive you. I'm not the one who got a knife in the arm."

"I'm not an invalid."

"Then you can take your car, and I'll take mine. No way am I getting stuck at your house without transportation."

He felt his stomach knot, hating the idea of letting her out of his sight until they were safely inside his house. So he made one last try.

"I'm not very far out of town. You can call a cab if you want to leave."

"I prefer to have my own transportation."

"Suit yourself," he muttered and told her what they were going to do.

First he stepped outside and breathed in the night air, looking and listening for anyone hiding in the darkness. Then he checked her car. After he'd satisfied himself that nobody was hunkered down in the back seat, he crossed the street and pulled his vehicle right behind hers.

Still wishing he was armed, he blinked his lights, then watched her step outside, slam the door, and dash to her car. Not until the door was locked behind her did he breathe out a little sigh.

He didn't like the idea of her following him. He wanted to stay in back of her where he could keep an eye on her. But he was the one who knew the way.

Probably he *was* a macho bastard, he decided, because he was grateful that she wasn't sitting next to him, watching him grimace in pain as he maneuvered the car through the dark streets.

At this time of night, with little traffic on the road, it was a fifteen-minute ride to his house. The whole way over he kept one eye on the rearview mirror.

His hands clenched the wheel as he thought about her taking the opportunity to slip away into the darkness. But to his profound relief, she stayed with him, following him up the long driveway to the old house that he'd picked because he liked the solitude. Now he was aware that the isolated location might make him vulnerable to attack.

Damn! When he'd come back to St. Stephens to find out who was making trouble for Lee Tillman, he hadn't been thinking he was going to get personally involved. He was thinking about it now as he stared around at the darkened fields that stretched away on either side of the house. A line of trees was just visible about twenty yards behind the structure, where Turtle Creek marked the back of the property.

He cut the engine, stepped out of the SUV and waited for Sara to join him on the sidewalk that led from the driveway to the front porch.

He hadn't been home since early in the day, and all the lights were off, leaving the house as a dark, shadowy mass hulking under the dim light from the three-quarter moon.

Sara stayed three paces behind him as he climbed the steps and crossed the porch. He unlocked the front door and stepped inside so he could switch on the hall light, then the porch.

Assuming she would follow him, he walked down the hall, turning on more lights as he went.

Now that he'd brought her home, he was feeling awkward. He was also looking around at the slightly shabby furniture he'd rented along with the place, wondering what she thought about it. He stifled the impulse to dash into the kitchen to see if he'd left a bunch of dishes in the sink. Probably not. He was pretty neat, by male standards.

"Do you want anything to eat or drink?" he asked.

She scuffed her foot against the worn beige carpet. "No thanks."

"The guest bedroom is upstairs. The bed's made, and towels are in the closet in the bathroom," he continued, still trying to play the gracious host, then added, "Maybe we should both get some rest."

"Yes. Thanks."

She was keeping her comments to a minimum and keeping her face averted from his. Probably she was remembering the intensity that had flared between them back at her house. He knew the best thing was to give her some breathing space.

He led her upstairs, showed her the bedroom at the front of the house and showed her the bathroom. Then he quickly withdrew into his own room and closed the door, keeping out of her way while she got ready for bed, wondering if she was going to turn down the covers or keep her clothes on and lie on top of the spread.

While she was in the bathroom, he took his Sig .40 out of the nightstand drawer and loaded it.

He started to put on his shoulder holster, but because of his injured arm thought better of it. He simply slipped the weapon into the holster and laid it beside him on the bed.

Feeling more secure—at least in the weapons department—he got out the special Randolph first-aid kit with its little jar of magic salve, the formula provided by Thorn Devereaux, one of the more unique individuals working for the company.

He could hear water running in the bathroom down the hall. Trying to block out the distraction, he removed the bandage and inspected the wound, then slathered on the salve, feeling an immediate warmth as it went to work on his sliced flesh. By the time he'd applied more gauze, the house was quiet.

After slipping off his shoes, he picked up the holstered gun and padded back down the stairs to his office, where he checked the answering machine.

There were four messages. The first was from Police Chief Hempstead who was reporting back on his conversation with Dana Eustice. His impressions matched Alex's own. As far as he could tell, Ms. Eustice didn't seem worried about Lee Tillman.

It was pretty neighborly of Hempstead to go to this much trouble. Alex was now in his debt, although not too deeply.

His caller ID told him that the other three calls were all from pay phones. The first two were hang-ups.

When he pressed the button to retrieve the third call, a familiar voice came on the line.

"Alex? Where the hell are you, Alex? I'm away from home and I don't have your cell phone number."

It was Lee!

"I need to talk to you. But I'm not going to leave a message on an answering machine."

No. Stay on the line, Alex silently screamed. The order did no good.

The connection snapped off, and Alex stood there cursing. He punched the replay button and listened to the call again, trying to pick up clues. First he focused on Lee's raspy voice. It sounded like Lee Tillman, but it could be someone imitating him. The person who had killed Lee or who was holding him for ransom. Or maybe the kidnapper was standing there with a gun trained on Lee.

Damn! If he only had Tillman's voice on a previous tape, he could send the two messages in for voice analysis. Even Lee's own machine had a computer-generated voice.

After pacing to the window, Alex came back to the desk and checked the times on the caller ID.

He'd assumed all of the calls had come from Lee. But now he noticed all three had come in after his fight with the intruder. Suppose someone knew about that and was checking to see if he'd arrived home safely?

The speculation got him wondering again if Lee's problem was tied to Sara's problem.

Frustrated, he ran a hand through his hair. He needed to think. He needed to sleep. But he was still too keyed up. And too aware of the woman upstairs in his guest bedroom.

He hadn't slept with anyone else in the house since he'd asked Cindy to leave. And now here was Sara occupying the spare bedroom.

Cindy. Sara.

His mind switched gears, from missing persons to interpersonal relations. He couldn't stop himself from juxtaposing the two women. Cindy represented the failure of his marriage. Well, more than that, actually.

He'd had a few sessions with a therapist to try and sort it out, and the shrink had assured him it wasn't a failure on his part. He had no control over his wife's behavior. Making a commitment to one man hadn't worked for her, and there was probably no way he could have made it work.

But deep down he couldn't help believing that it had been his fault. If he'd been a better husband, or a better lover, she wouldn't have needed to turn to anyone else.

He gritted his teeth, then deliberately relaxed his jaw. There was no point in giving himself a headache to go with his throbbing arm.

He switched from Cindy to an equally disturbing subject—Sara. She represented something else. At least the Sara from the long-ago encounter in the car. That was back in the days when Alex Shane had been God's gift to women. When he could have any chick he wanted. When he was arrogant in his knowledge of how easily he could please them, how easily he could get what he wanted from them.

It must be one reason why he was so wound up with her now. She represented the good old days. But there was another aspect to the picture, too. He'd once thought he loved Cindy, and she'd betrayed him. Did the disaster with Cindy influence his thinking now? Was it making him suspect that Sara was holding back information? In the back of his mind, he was waiting for more confirmation that his judgment sucked—at least with regard to women.

He simply wasn't capable of logical thought, or of sorting out the emotions churning through him.

Striding down the hall to the kitchen, he switched on the light by the back door. After opening the dead bolt, he stepped out onto the low wooden deck. In the far corner was a hot tub. When he'd first looked at the house, he'd been intrigued with the idea of sitting in it out here—in the privacy of his rented acres.

He'd used the tub several times a week since he'd moved in, and knew that the hot water would soothe his aching body—although keeping the injured arm dry was probably a good idea.

He glanced back toward the house, thinking that it might not be such a bright idea to get naked out here when he had company upstairs. Particularly when his houseguest was Sara Ellen Delaney. Then he reminded himself how anxious she'd been to avoid him. He'd bet he wasn't going to see her until morning.

With a shrug, he turned on the gas heater and the water jets but left the underwater lights dark.

Then he pulled a towel from the locker against the house, shucked off his clothes and tossed them on a white resin chair. The night air was chilly, and he stood for several moments, enjoying the feel of it against his naked skin before he stepped into the heated water.

The bubbling warmth enveloped his body as he sank onto one of the seats and leaned back against the side of the tub, stretching out his arms against the top ledge and sighing with pleasure as he let the liquid heat soothe his bruises.

Head tipped back, he stared up at the stars, marveling at how much brighter they were than in the city. He spent ten minutes staring at the heavens. Then, yanking his mind back to earth, he forced himself to focus on the mystery of Lee Tillman and the two attacks on Sara, trying to figure out how they fit together.

He'd been acquainted with Lee Tillman for a good part of his life, and he'd made certain judgments about the man. Now he realized that he hardly knew him. He was a small man, with a small man's built-in inferiority complex. He liked to give orders and insisted on having things his way. When he liked you, he could be a good friend—on his terms. But he had a secret life Alex had never suspected. And a pornographic art collection that added another dimension to his personality.

Was Lee using him? Or had Lee gotten himself into deep trouble? Perhaps because of some unusual sexual encounter, Alex reasoned. And what about Sara? How did she fit into the equation?

He'd had a long hard day, and as the hot water relaxed him, his eyes drifted closed. He was thinking that he might be able to get some sleep after all, when a noise by the back door startled him.

A figure stood silhouetted in the doorway. For several charged seconds he cursed his own negligence at leaving his gun on the chair on the other side of the deck.

Then he took in the outline of the slender feminine figure and realized that it was Sara, barefoot, dressed in a
T-shirt and shorts.

"Damn," he muttered under his breath.

"Alex?" she asked, her voice not quite steady.

He sat up straighter in the water. "I'm in the hot tub.
Not exactly dressed for company. What are you doing
here?"

She lifted her arm, then let it fall back to her side. "I
couldn't sleep."

"I know the feeling."

"Alex—" She broke off abruptly.

"Yeah?"

She didn't answer for several seconds, and he figured
she'd decided that coming out here was a bad idea.

In the moonlight, he saw her lean back against the door
frame. "I've been tossing around in your guest bed upstairs, thinking that I haven't been—" She stopped, sucked
in a breath, then let it out in a rush. "I guess I should
admit that I've been lying to you."

Chapter Six

Alex started to surge out of the water, then he remembered he was naked. He sat back down.

He'd been unconsciously waiting for this, he realized. Waiting to find out that she wasn't playing it straight with him.

"Maybe you'd better clarify that statement." Although he'd tried to keep his voice steady, he was pretty sure she'd caught his reaction.

"I don't mean I stabbed you in the back," she murmured.

"What *do* you mean?"

She stepped out onto the deck and onto one of the resin chairs, and he saw her fold her arms under her breasts.

"You asked me questions. I didn't like the way you were prying into my life and...I didn't want to think about the answers, so I ignored some stuff."

"Like what?"

"You asked if I knew that guy. The one who was in my house."

Again he felt the tension gathering in the pit of his stomach. "Do you know him?"

"Well, not his name."

"You're sure?"

"Of course I'm sure!" She huffed out a breath. "But I've seen him around town. I mean, I think he might have been following me. Him and…some other guys."

"Someone's been tailing you? Consistently?"

"Not all the time. All I can tell you is that I've started noticing these guys. Not anybody I'd recognize."

He gave her time to spell out more details. When he didn't speak, she unfolded her arms and turned her palms up. "I don't know if you could actually say they're following me. But they're *there*."

"Anything distinguishing about them?"

"Well, I don't like to put people into categories."

"Now's not the time to be politically correct."

"All of them are white. They all have a kind of redneck look."

"What does that mean?"

She laughed. "I don't know. Like they didn't get enough protein for adequate brain development when they were growing up. Like they think the world owes them something they're not getting. I've never seen them wearing anything besides jeans and a faded T-shirt, with maybe a plaid shirt over the top. And big boots. Sometimes they have on baseball caps so I can't see their faces. Most of them have short hair. At least it doesn't stick out much under their caps. There's nothing more I can be precise about."

"Thank you for leveling with me." He cleared his throat. "Now, why do you think they're interested in you?"

She scuffed her foot against the boards of the deck. "Are you naked in there?"

"Yeah." He didn't add that despite the nature of the conversation they were having, he was aroused.

"Maybe I'd better go in."

"Don't use my state of undress as an excuse for bailing out."

When she didn't answer, he prompted, "I can't help you unless you tell me the whole story."

He saw her heave a large sigh. "Maybe…maybe it has something to do with my father."

That was the last thing he'd expected. "Like how?"

"He's gotten into some trouble recently."

"Why don't you tell me about it."

"It's hard to talk about it."

"Trouble with the police?" he suddenly asked, recalling something she'd said back at her house.

Her head came up. "What do you know about that?"

"I just remembered that you thought about calling the police on me but then you changed your mind. I figured you had a reason."

She shrugged.

He'd felt as if he was making progress, and she'd shut him out again. He tapped his fingers against the rim of the tub, thinking that he might get further if she wasn't talking to a naked man.

Yeah, maybe that was making her nervous. It wasn't doing anything for his concentration either, not when he kept imagining what it would be like if she took off her clothes and climbed in here with him.

Resolutely, he pushed that little fantasy out of his mind and cleared his throat. "Listen, why don't I get dressed? Then we can have a more civilized conversation."

"Okay."

"You could make us some hot chocolate."

"You drink hot chocolate?" she asked, sounding surprised.

"What? You only picture me with a macho drink like bourbon on the rocks?"

She laughed. "Something like that."

"Go on in. The mix is in the first cabinet you come to on the right. The kettle is on the stove."

She hurried into the kitchen, and he waited until he saw a light on before climbing out of the tub and grabbing his towel.

He dried off and pulled on his jeans. Then in the laundry room he found a clean T-shirt.

When he moved his arm in the light, he caught a flash of white. The bandage. He'd forgotten about getting cut. Gingerly he felt the wound through the gauze. It was healing remarkably fast. Other Randolph agents had told him of the salve's miraculous powers, but he'd only half believed them. Now he simply grinned in silent agreement.

He thought about taking a quick trip down the hall to his office for the background information he'd dug on Sara this morning. It had included something about her father. Now Alex couldn't even remember the guy's name.

Well, if she didn't tell him what he wanted to know, he'd do more digging on his own.

By the time he entered the kitchen, he saw Sara standing by the counter. She'd only turned on the low light over the sink, but the illumination caught the strands of her hair and turned them to gold. She stood with her back partially to him, her head bent as she stirred chocolate mix into a mug. He wondered if she was keeping her face averted because she wished she hadn't agreed to the discussion.

He paused near the doorway, shoving his hands into his pockets as he searched for some way to ease into the conversation.

She'd set a plate of Oreo cookies on the round wooden table.

"I see you found my stash of cookies," he observed.

Forced to acknowledge his presence, she looked up. "I hope you don't mind."

"No. I was thinking they'd go perfectly with the hot chocolate," he answered as he pulled out a chair and sat down. She brought over the second mug and seated herself.

He wrapped his hands around the crockery, absorbing the warmth, then decided to take the direct approach. "So your father's in some kind of trouble?"

She looked up for the first time, meeting his eyes. "His life hasn't been easy. It's taken a turn for the worse."

"He's sick?"

"No. He worked for White and Sandler."

White and Sandler, a manufacturer of power tools, had been one of the main industries on the Eastern Shore. But its business had fallen off over the past few years, and the plant that had provided jobs for so many of the area's people had considerably reduced its workforce.

"He got laid off?" Alex asked.

"Yes. He's got a small pension and some social security, but it's not enough."

Alex kept his gaze level, remembering that she gave her dad two hundred dollars a month. He wanted to know more, but he might have to go around the barn to get it. "My old man had some problems, too. Problems with his eyesight, actually. He didn't want to admit he was losing his vision. One night he plowed his boat into a bridge piling and killed himself. I was nine at the time. My brother Billy was seven."

Compassion warmed her gaze. "Oh, I'm sorry."

"My mom was short of money. She did her best to raise us. But we were...pretty wild kids. My mom didn't have many marketable skills. She'd married my dad out of high school and worked as a maid for several families in the area, including Lee Tillman. He saw she was going under, and he gave her extra hours when she needed them and paid her more than the going rate, too. So that's part of the debt I owe him.''

Her eyes widened. Then she said, ''You seem to have turned out okay.''

''It was touch-and-go. I finally realized that I was heading for a dead-end life.'' He shifted in his seat. ''Lee did more than help my mom. He offered to pay my tuition at the University of Maryland. I've paid him back what he spent on me.''

Again he saw her shocked reaction.

''He made the same offer to my brother. Billy turned him down, got into worse trouble than when he was a teenager. He did a few years in jail. He's out now, and most likely looking for trouble to get into again.''

''I'm sorry.''

''So am I.''

To fill the silence that descended, they each picked up their mugs and sipped the chocolate. Alex reached for a cookie and took several bites.

''Is your mother still alive?'' she finally asked.

''She died.''

''Mine, too,'' Sara murmured.

''So what about your father?'' he asked, steering the conversation back where he wanted it.

Sara sucked in a breath and let it out in a rush. ''He's probably been an alcoholic since I was a little girl. I didn't know it back then. He kept it to weekends. I guess he drank because my mom liked to make sure he understood his failings. We had a pretty dysfunctional family.''

''In my work, I've discovered that most families are dysfunctional.''

He watched as she reached for a cookie and began rolling it around the plate.

"Mom had a lot of gripes. About our income, about how Dad didn't take care of the house, about how we never had a decent car. But her biggest complaint was that he had a low sperm count, and he couldn't give her any children." She made a small sound. "Low sperm count—one of my earliest verbal memories."

Alex took that in. "But you..."

"I'm adopted."

"Sounds like you were plunked into the middle of a messy situation."

"No! I mean, both my parents loved me. But I didn't know how to cope with the friction between them." She moved restlessly in her seat. "I feel guilty about airing dirty laundry in public."

"This isn't public. It's with the security expert who wants to figure out who's coming after you."

She nodded.

"So you think that someone who's mad at your father might be looking for a way to hurt him through you?"

"I guess it's possible. At least you got me thinking about it."

"Yeah. Do you know who he's, uh, angered?"

"Chief Hempstead has some disorderly-conduct reports. That's all I know."

He followed the pointed question with another. "Did your father have any reason to be angry with Lee Tillman?"

"They didn't get along," she clipped out.

"Why?"

She pushed back her chair and stood up. "This conversation is making me uneasy."

He stood too, facing her across the table. "I'm sorry if it seems like prying. I'm trying to help you."

"Are you? Or are you trying to figure out what happened to Lee?"

"Both."

"Well, I feel like you've manipulated me."

"How?"

"By telling me about your background to get me to cough up information about mine."

He shrugged.

"Is that a technique you learned in the detective squad? Identify with the suspect to encourage confessions?"

That was exactly the technique he'd been using, but he was damned if he was going to say so. "I thought you'd feel more comfortable talking about your background if you knew mine," he allowed.

"Right," she murmured, then picked up her mug and set it down with a thunk in the sink. Without giving him another look, she exited the kitchen.

He watched her leave, feeling a mixture of emotions: regret, anger, self-disgust. He didn't know if her father was connected to Lee's disappearance. And he didn't know how the lowlife guys following her around fit into the equation.

The only thing he was sure of was that he didn't want her to be a suspect. He wanted her to be totally innocent of any wrongdoing. And at the same time, that desire made him feel edgy. It didn't matter what he wanted for her. What mattered was finding out what happened to Lee. And if he could solve Sara Delaney's problems while he was doing it, that would be a bonus.

He carried his own cup to the sink, rinsed them both and set them in the dishwasher. Then he turned off the lights and made a check of the doors and windows, although he already knew they were secure.

He might have gone into his office and started poring over his usual databases—this time looking for information on Reid Delaney. But his arm was starting to throb again, and he knew that despite the magic salve, he'd better give the knife wound a chance to heal.

Silently acknowledging that he was stalling, he stood at the bottom of the steps, looking up and listening. He could hear nothing, which probably meant Sara had already turned in for the night.

Of course, he'd thought she'd turned in earlier.

He didn't want to picture her lying in the double bed in his guest room. But he couldn't stop himself from conjuring up an image of her snuggled under the covers, her blond hair spread across the pillow. He'd like to put her in a sexy nightgown, as well. One that exposed a lot of creamy skin and showed the darker circles of her nipples through the cups of the bodice.

When he found himself getting hard again, he cursed under his breath. She was probably still wearing her T-shirt and shorts, in case they ran into each other in the hall at night.

Still, he couldn't banish the image of the sheer, sexy gown revealing her slender curves.

He gritted his teeth, then climbed the stairs, his arousal increasing the closer he got to her door. He strode past her room and into his. He undressed swiftly, leaving on his briefs. Slipping under the covers, he lay with his hands stacked behind his head, trying to think about Lee Tillman's disappearance. But the woman down the hall kept working her way to the forefront of his mind.

Was she lying awake, thinking about him?

Yeah, sure. She was probably wishing that she'd kept her mouth shut about her family.

He closed his eyes, then went into a relaxation routine he'd learned from Kathryn Kelley, one of the psychologists at 43 Light Street. In addition to her private practice, Kathryn did special programs for the men and women at Randolph Security, and her techniques had helped him deal with some of the tension that his divorce had created.

It helped tonight, too. One moment he had filled his mind with soft blue clouds; in the next, he had drifted off to a blessedly calm sleep.

The phone woke him around six in the morning just as it had the day before. Hoping it was Lee, he reached for the receiver.

"Hello."

"Alex, thank God."

"Who is this?"

"Emmett Bandy."

The real estate agent's voice sounded odd, as if he was whispering.

"What's wrong?"

"I'm talking on my cell phone in the bathroom," the man answered. "You were asking people questions about Lee Tillman yesterday. And I heard through the grapevine that he hired you to protect him. Well, I'm the one who needs protecting. He's here, in my office, threatening me with a gun. He says I'd better give him his money or else."

Alex swore. "Your office downtown?"

"Yes. You've got to come down here. Otherwise he's going to do something he'll regret later."

Alex weighed his options. He'd seen Lee mad. He knew that the guy had a hair-trigger temper. If he also had a gun, that was bad. "Have you called the police?" he asked.

"No. And don't you do it!"

"Why not?"

"If you don't want Lee to get into trouble, you'd better not get the cops involved."

"I'll be there as quick as I can."

"Hurry up. And park in one of the spaces behind the building. The back door's open."

While he'd been speaking Alex had been climbing back into his jeans, and pulling on his socks and running shoes. Next, he dragged his T-shirt over his head, then strapped on his shoulder holster and stuffed the Sig inside. After shrugging into a light jacket, he stepped into the hall and found Sara standing beside her door looking uncertainly in his direction. "Alex? Who was that? Was it Lee? Have you located him?"

"Not Lee. But…I've got a situation here. That was someone who says he knows where Lee is. I've got to go check it out."

"Now?"

"Yes. You stay here." After a pause, he asked, "Are you familiar with firearms?"

She nodded. "My dad made sure I could handle a gun."

He returned to his room and retrieved his Glock model 30. When he handed her the weapon, she held it down toward the floor while she checked to see if it was loaded.

"Don't open the door to anyone except me or the police."

"The police?"

"I'm not expecting them."

"Okay," she answered, and he wished like hell that he wasn't running out on her. But he was working for Lee, and if the man was on the verge of doing something stupid—like killing Emmett Bandy—he had to stop him. More than that, this was his chance to find out what the hell had been going on since Lee's frantic phone call.

Maybe he was going to find out that his employer had lost his marbles. At least that was how Bandy was making it sound.

"I'll be back as soon as I can," he said.

YESTERDAY MORNING when he'd left the house, he'd headed toward Lee's estate, The Refuge. Now he turned toward town, taking advantage of the sparse traffic to put the accelerator to the floor.

As he drove, he went over the message in his mind. Bandy had said Lee was threatening him but he didn't want the authorities to know about it. That sounded as if the two men were into some sort of dirty business together. Had Lee gotten angry with his partner?

Alex shook his head. He didn't like this.

He made it to the restored area in twelve minutes. As instructed, he pulled around back of Bandy's office and parked beside a car that was already there. It wasn't one of Lee's vehicles, as far as he knew. Probably Bandy's.

Walking around it, he headed toward the back of the building, then tried the door. As promised, it was open.

Alex stepped into the dim interior, expecting to hear angry voices.

Quietly he tiptoed down the dark hall, the silence around him taking on an eerie quality. Reaching under his jacket, he unholstered his Sig and held it down by his right leg as he moved along the wall, alert for trouble.

He found it in Bandy's office.

The real estate agent was slumped backward in his desk. His left arm was still in a sling, but that wasn't his most pressing health problem at the moment. Blood had spread from a small hole in his skull, dripping down his face and onto his shirt.

Alex moved forward, touching the man's neck.

Emmett Bandy was dead.

Alex grimaced as he debated what the hell to do now. Bending again, he examined the entry wound. It was small, like from a twenty-two maybe. He followed the angle of Bandy's head and found the bullet embedded in the metal door frame in back of the man.

As he looked at the slug, his mind returned to the phone conversation.

Someone had called him. He'd thought it was Bandy. But the voice had been low and distorted. Maybe it was someone who had just killed him and wanted Alex Shane to find the body.

The scenario was disturbing because it would mean that Bandy had already been dead when the call was made. Killed by Lee? Or someone who wanted Alex to think that Lee had done it?

That meant it had to be someone who knew about Lee's disappearance. His mind immediately flashed to Sara.

Could she have made a phone call while he was asleep and told an accomplice about the case? He didn't think so, but he couldn't be sure.

He muttered a curse under his breath. He wanted to stop jumping to suspicious conclusions about her, but that didn't seem possible. Every time he got the chance, he thought the worst of her.

But she wasn't Cindy, he reminded himself. He couldn't condemn her because of what his former wife had done to him.

He looked around the office. Maybe there were some clues here that would help sort things out. He'd be careful not to obstruct a police investigation. He just wanted to know what was going on.

He pulled a handkerchief from his pocket and held it in his hand as he opened the door on the left. It was a closet.

Seconds later, he heard a noise in back of him and whirled, his weapon raised.

Then he saw who was blocking the office doorway.

"Police, freeze." The order came from Clark Hempstead, who was standing with his own weapon aimed right at Alex.

Chapter Seven

"Put the gun on the table—slowly. Then raise your hands," Hempstead said.

Knowing that compliance was his only choice, Alex obeyed.

A million thoughts went rapidly through his head as he followed orders, his movements slow and easy. As easy as they could be when he was struggling to keep his hands from shaking.

Lord, he'd been a fool not to get out of here as soon as he'd seen that Emmett Bandy was dead. Maybe he'd been a fool to come down here in the first place. But he'd shown up and he'd stuck around, so he could get caught at a murder scene holding a damn gun. Hempstead had probable cause to believe he'd committed the crime and now he was going to be arrested for a murder he hadn't committed.

If he didn't end up with a bullet hole in his own chest. Which was a distinct possibility, because the chief was damn well going to make sure that Alex Shane didn't shoot him and make his escape.

"Step away from the weapon."

Alex instantly followed that clipped order, too.

The chief waited until he'd backed off, then reached for

the Sig, his own weapon still trained on Alex. Never taking his eyes off the murder suspect, he put the automatic on the desk.

When Alex saw him reach for the pair of handcuffs clipped to his weapon belt, he wanted to scream out a protest of his innocence. But he kept silent.

"You're under arrest. Hands behind your back," Hempstead clipped out.

Alex obeyed, his stomach in knots as Hempstead snapped the cuffs into place. The chief sighed, a sad sound that seemed to fill the small room. A sigh of disappointment in Alex Shane.

Alex felt a surge of something sick and tight inside his chest. Slowly he turned to face the man who had arrested him half a dozen times during his wild teenage years. "I know what this looks like. But I didn't do it," he said.

"Uh-huh," Hempstead muttered, then asked, "Any other weapons on you?" Pushing Alex's legs slightly wider than his shoulders, he began to pat him down.

"No," Alex answered, thankful he'd left the Glock home with Sara.

Oh God, he thought, suddenly. Sara. He'd told her he'd be back soon. Now…

He was silently cursing as Hempstead whipped out his cell phone and called the state police.

The sick feeling in Alex's chest increased. The state police. Of course. This wasn't like the old TV series, *Mayberry RFD,* where the sheriff handled everything. Hempstead wouldn't tackle a murder investigation on his own. He didn't have the resources or the experience.

Alex tried to make himself numb as he listened to the cold, hard description of the crime—the shooting victim and the suspect who had been apprehended with a gun in his hand.

When the chief finished, Alex looked him directly in the eye. "I know it's hard to believe at the moment, but somebody very carefully set me up."

"Son, save it for the detectives. They can Mirandize you, since they're going to do the questioning. Right now I've got to inventory the stuff in your pockets and lock you in the back of my car."

Alex's temper flared at the man's patronizing tone. "I think I have a right to talk."

"You'd be smart to have a lawyer with you."

"I can do that later. I want you to know what happened. I got a call from Bandy asking me to come down here. Or maybe it was somebody imitating Bandy's voice. What are *you* doing here, by the way? Somebody called you with a hot tip, right?"

"Yeah. I got a call," he allowed, his tone flat.

"From whom?"

He shrugged. "Whoever it was told me to get down here on the double."

"Someone who killed Bandy a few minutes ago then watched to make sure I arrived on the scene," Alex added, before continuing quickly. "You can check for powder burns on my hands. You won't find any. You can check the caliber of my weapon. It's a Sig .40. I think Bandy was shot with a twenty-two. I found the bullet lodged in the door frame over there." Since his hands were cuffed behind his back, he nodded his head toward the slug and thanked God that it hadn't gone out the window and into the night.

For the first time, he saw a flicker of hope on Hempstead's lined visage. But all he said was, "You can tell all that to the state troopers."

Alex nodded, wishing again that he'd left Bandy's office as soon as he'd seen the man was dead.

As he sat in the police car, with Hempstead in the front seat, he thought that at least it was parked behind the building, not in front. And it was early enough in the morning that nobody he knew was likely to come strolling by. The arrest would hit the news soon enough, but the public didn't have to see him handcuffed and humiliated.

Closing his eyes, he struggled to focus on something else—and dredged up the helpful information that in Maryland you couldn't get bond on a murder charge. And that there would be no use asking to have ballistics tests expedited. Everybody wanted their tests expedited, and the system was backed up.

He was still contemplating his immediate future when the state police took him into custody twenty minutes later. It didn't matter that he'd been a detective with the Howard County P.D. He was a murder suspect now. When they arrived at the police barracks, he was booked, photographed and fingerprinted like any other criminal.

But at least he knew the ropes. He made sure they checked for powder burns on his hands. And he also made sure they checked his weapon and noted that it hadn't been fired recently.

After one of the detectives assigned to the case had read him his rights, he decided that he'd gone it alone long enough and maybe he ought to have a lawyer present before he said anything else.

So he asked to call his attorney and dialed the Randolph Security emergency number.

As per the law, they let him do it in private, in a small, windowless room. He breathed a little sigh of relief when it turned out that Lucas Somerville, one of his friends, was manning the line.

"Problems?" Lucas asked.

"I'm in a bit of a jam, yeah. Actually, I've been arrested for murder, and I need a lawyer."

He was glad that Lucas didn't swear, didn't raise his voice as he asked for details. He gave a few, then Lucas cut in, "Randolph Security will back you all the way on this."

"I figured you would. But it's nice to hear it."

"We'll have Dan Cassidy down there in the next few hours."

The name and the time frame sent a wave of relief crashing through Alex.

Dan Cassidy was a good man to have on your side. Until a couple of months ago, he'd been a state's attorney, the equivalent of a district attorney in other regions of the country. But he'd grown frustrated with the backlog of cases jamming the Baltimore court system and had been looking for a change of pace. Since Dan's wife, Sabrina, ran the lobby shop at 43 Light Street, he was already hooked into the network of friends who had offices in the building. When he'd put out the word that he was available, Randolph Security, which often worked closely with the Light Street group, hired him immediately.

Alex hung up feeling better than he had a few minutes earlier. It gave him a tremendous boost to know that Lucas believed him, with no questions asked. And he knew that Dan Cassidy was the perfect choice for a defense attorney—a lawyer intimately familiar with the Maryland criminal system.

The sense of relief lasted until he thought about Sara again. She was at his house, probably wondering where he was.

At least, as a former cop, he knew the one phone call rule was just a myth made up by mystery novelists. So he asked to call home. This time, a uniformed officer stood with him while he dialed and waited with his heart pounding as the phone rang—once, twice, three times.

Finally, his answering machine picked up, and he heard his own voice.

"This is Alex Shane. I'm not available to take your call right now, but please leave a message at the sound of the beep."

Yeah, Alex thought. *I'm not available because I'm in the pokey being charged with murder.*

The message was short, but he felt his blood pressure climb while he waited for the tone.

Then he practically shouted into the phone. "Sara, are you there? Sara? Pick up, dammit."

When she answered, he felt the breath whoosh out of his lungs.

"Alex, what's wrong? Where are you?"

The sound of her voice made his throat clog. It was several seconds before he could say, "I ran into a little problem. I'm at the state police barracks."

When he heard her indrawn breath, he closed his eyes, although the maneuver only gave him the illusion of privacy.

"What happened?" she asked.

"I'll give you the condensed version. That call I got this morning—I thought it was from Emmett Bandy. At least it sounded like Bandy. When I got to his office, he was sitting at his desk with a bullet through his brain."

She gasped, but he went on quickly. "Hempstead walked in on me with my gun drawn."

"Oh God, Alex. What's going to happen?"

She sounded scared. She sounded genuinely concerned for him, which made him answer in a clipped voice, "I'm under arrest for Bandy's murder."

There was a moment of silence during which he died a thousand deaths.

Then she said quietly, "They must know you didn't do it."

"It would have been better if I hadn't been holding a gun."

"Yes," she murmured, then, "What can I do to help you?"

As it had with Lucas, the offer of support buoyed him. "My firm, Randolph Security, is sending a lawyer down from Baltimore. Dan Cassidy. He knows the ropes."

"Okay. Good."

"Sara, nothing's changed since what happened last night," he said cautiously, not wanting to say too much since she'd told him specifically that she didn't want to get the police involved after she'd been attacked.

"But—"

"I'm in the middle of the police station."

"All right, I understand."

"Probably it would be a good idea for you to go to your father's." His hand clenched the receiver. He'd taken her home to keep her safe and he'd made a mess of that particular job. Just as he'd made a mess of the scene at Bandy's.

"Can...I bring you anything?"

"No!" he said sharply, thinking that the last thing he wanted was for her to see him behind bars. "Dan will take care of things. I'll let you know when I'm out of here."

"When will that be?"

He sighed. "I don't know." He didn't add that if his luck went the wrong way, he could be here for months.

SARA SAT HUDDLED in Alex's office. She'd been in the kitchen making coffee, thinking he'd be back soon. When the phone rang, she hadn't been sure whether it was all right to answer it. Then she'd heard his voice shouting at her, and she'd snatched up the receiver. What he'd told her had been like getting hit with a bucket of freezing water.

Alex. In jail. Arrested for murder.

He'd hung up, leaving her numb and disoriented. Finally, she roused herself, but it was still difficult to believe what he had said. When he'd left the house a few hours ago, although he hadn't said it, she was sure that he was going out to take care of an emergency. Apparently he'd walked into a situation he wasn't prepared for.

Alex had told her not to come down to the police barracks, but she couldn't just sit here doing nothing. Glancing at the clock, she saw it was before eight, which meant that the network talk shows would still be on. She knew the segments were interspersed with local newscasts and wondered if she could get more details of the arrest.

The problem was, she couldn't find a television on the ground floor. She climbed the steps to the second story, then hesitated in the hall outside his bedroom, where she spied a small TV on the dresser. It felt like an invasion of Alex's privacy to step into his room.

It was neat. There were no personal possessions in evidence, no pictures, knicknacks. The bedside table was stacked with books, however. Mostly nonfiction: true crime, military history, a new biography of Dwight Eisenhower.

Her eyes slid to the bed. The sheets were tangled, suggesting that he hadn't slept well. Neither had she.

She turned on the television and found the Salisbury channel, which was affiliated with one of the major networks. Standing with her arms clutching her shoulders, she waited for the commercials to finish. She sat on the edge of the bed, unconsciously smoothing her hand over the spread. Then the network broke for a local segment.

"This just in," the blond newscaster reported in a breathy voice. "An employee of a Baltimore security firm has been arrested in connection with a homicide in downtown St. Stephens."

Sara's eyes remained glued to the television screen. She saw the exterior of Emmett Bandy's office, state police cars with flashing lights, yellow crime-scene tape.

"Alex Shane, apparently on assignment in St. Stephens, was arrested early this morning in the office of real estate owner Emmett Bandy. Although details are still sketchy, it is reported that the unarmed Bandy had been shot. Shane was apprehended still holding his weapon."

Sara made a small sound of protest. She might be unsure of her own relationship with Alex. She might be upset that he still didn't trust her. But she knew with bone-deep conviction that he hadn't killed Emmett Bandy in cold blood.

As she watched, she caught a picture of Clark Hempstead talking to several uniformed officers. But he waved away a reporter who approached him with a microphone.

In the background, she could see that a small group of rubberneckers had gathered. She recognized a number of the locals, including Dana Eustice, Lee Tillman's girlfriend. That was interesting. Had she simply happened along, or did she know something about Lee?

That line of speculation was cut off when Sara spotted several men standing apart from the others. She sucked in a sharp breath as she stared at their plaid shirts, their baseball caps. It was them! The guys who had been following her around. She had never gotten a good look at them before, but here they were, right on television for her inspection.

She studied their faces, thinking that she didn't recognize anybody. Then one of them turned to say something to his friends, and she froze.

For a moment she had thought it was Alex. Then she focused on his features and saw that it was just someone who looked very similar.

Sara felt gooseflesh rise on her neck as she remembered Alex telling her about his brother. She stared at the group on the TV, thinking how she'd told Alex about these men—and now she was wondering if his brother was one of them.

"SO NOW THAT YOU understand your rights, let's go over the events of the morning again," said Detective Jerry Plymouth, the guy who had been assigned to this case.

"Okay," Alex agreed. He was sitting in a small, windowless room with gray walls and a battered metal table. Dan Cassidy sat next to him, wearing a crisp blue suit that looked as if it had just come off the rack.

A rumpled-looking Detective Plymouth was on the other side of the table. As Alex sized up the opposition, he felt himself taking control of the situation.

Plymouth was young, and his experience was limited to one of Maryland's rural counties. Alex had five years' experience in detective work in a county with a large metropolitan area. He'd carried out his share of interrogations, and now that the tables were turned on him, he knew what to do and say—and what to avoid.

He eyed the thick folder Plymouth had carried into the interrogation room. Nice prop, he thought, since he knew they didn't have much of a case against him. Only his inconvenient presence at the scene of the crime—with his weapon drawn.

He sat up straight in his chair, made direct eye contact with the detective and said, "I didn't kill anybody. And you can use all the brilliant ploys on me you like, but you're not going to get me to admit to a crime I didn't commit.''

Plymouth shifted in his chair. ''So tell me in your own words what happened this morning in Emmett Bandy's office.''

''All right,'' Alex agreed, starting back over the account he'd already given, sticking to the facts. He began with some background on why he'd come to St. Stephens—to find out who was threatening Lee Tillman. Then he went on to the man's disappearance, congratulating himself that he'd consulted Chief Hempstead about it right off the bat. Hempstead could back him up on that. Unless Hempstead was playing dirty pool, which he hoped was beneath the chief's dignity.

Maybe some of what he was thinking flashed in his eyes, because Plymouth was suddenly alert.

Forcing himself back to the facts, he explained about Bandy's frantic call and how he'd gone down to the real estate office expecting trouble. Which was why he'd had his gun drawn.

Then he went on to repeat what he'd told Hempstead, which was the same thing he'd said in his initial interview.

''I know your preliminary test for powder burns was negative,'' he said. ''I know the more extensive tests will come out the same way. I know I didn't fire my gun. Your tests will show that. And I know the bullet that exited Bandy's skull and ended up in the door frame is not from my weapon.''

When Plymouth tried to take back control of the interrogation, Alex sat calmly in his chair and let him use the techniques that had probably worked on scores of criminals.

After Plymouth had given it his best shot, Alex folded

his arms and said, "Your other problem is that you don't have a motive. I have no reason to kill Emmett Bandy. He called me for help. You'll find a record of that call in the phone company log. I didn't call him. He contacted me. But I think now that it was the killer imitating Bandy's voice.

"The call was made from Bandy's cell phone. You'll also find a record of another call made to Chief Hempstead, probably from a pay phone, probably right after I arrived at Bandy's office. Whoever it was wanted to make sure Hempstead would catch me there. So why don't you stop wasting your time trying to pin a murder on me that I didn't commit and start looking for the real killer?"

At that point, Dan Cassidy took over. "My client has been completely cooperative with you. He's got no motive for having murdered Emmett Bandy. And you won't find any evidence connecting him to the crime—other than that he was unfortunate enough to be on the scene because he was lured there."

"With a gun in his hand," Plymouth reminded everyone in the small, hot room.

"But not the murder weapon," Cassidy retorted. "A gun he brought along because he was called by a man who was fearful and begging for protection. I think it can be established pretty quickly that the bullet didn't come from his Sig. I was a prosecutor in this state for eighteen years, and I know damn well what you need to make a case. You don't have one."

As he listened to his lawyer's speech, taking in the quiet conviction in Dan's voice, Alex hoped he was projecting a calm exterior, even though his insides were twisting razor wire. He might have talked his own good game with Plymouth, but he understood that he'd gotten himself into a mess. He hadn't prayed in years, but now he said a silent prayer that Dan could get him out of it.

THE CRUNCH OF TIRES on the gravel driveway sent Sara rushing to the window. Although Alex had told her to go to her father's hours ago, she was still here, hoping that somehow he'd be released.

The man who'd brought his vehicle to a stop beside hers wasn't Alex, and she knew that she'd put herself in serious jeopardy by staying here.

Her heart started to pound as the guy opened the door of his SUV and climbed out. There was no use pretending she wasn't home. Men had been following her around. They knew her car, and it was in the driveway.

Worse, if they'd had the news on today, they knew that Alex wasn't home.

"Stupid. Stupid," she muttered as she darted down the hall to the office where she'd left the gun.

She was back at the front door in seconds, standing to the side in case the man coming up the porch steps started shooting through the wood panels.

Her breath rapid and shallow, she watched him through the crack where she'd pulled the curtains aside. He was holding a briefcase instead of a gun. A good sign.

He knocked on the door, then called out, "Ms. Delaney."

"Who is it?"

"Dan Cassidy, Alex's lawyer."

"Can you show me some identification?" she asked.

Through the crack in the curtains, she saw him reach into his back pocket and pull out his wallet. When he held it toward the window where she was peeking out, she felt a mixture of relief and chagrin.

She unbolted the door and swung it open. Standing face-to-face with the man was reassuring. He looked solid. He looked as if he knew what he was doing.

And when he stepped into the hall and closed the door behind him, he acted as if he owned the place.

"I thought Alex told you to go to your father's," he said as he marched into the living room and settled himself in an easy chair.

She took the couch opposite him. "I couldn't leave. I kept hoping he'd come back."

"Well, I'm working on that."

"What are his chances?"

"The evidence against him won't hold up. It's all a matter of how quickly I can get them to perform the necessary tests." He gave her an assessing look. "You didn't ask if I thought he was guilty."

"I know he's not."

"How?"

"He wouldn't shoot anyone in cold blood."

"You're sure of that?"

"Very sure."

He nodded. "Yeah, anybody who knows Alex knows what kind of man he is. Unfortunately, he got into a couple of scrapes with the police when he was a teenager."

"I thought a juvenile record was sealed."

"To the general public. Not to the police."

"Oh."

Cassidy had relaxed somewhat, but he still seemed to be considering what he wanted to say next. "How well do you know Alex?" he asked.

She looked down at her hands, then up again. "We knew each other slightly as teenagers," she answered, giving this man information that she hadn't even been willing to share with Alex. "But we hadn't been in contact in years. Then we ran into each other again because he's investigating Lee Tillman's disappearance. Or whatever it is. Alex thinks I'm involved somehow."

She was aware of the man across from her listening carefully, weighing her words, judging her veracity.

"Are you?" he asked quietly.

"Not in the way he thinks! I'm Lee's accountant. He and I are friendly, but I don't have any idea what happened to him. Probably Alex told you that men have been following me around, that somebody tried to run me down. And somebody broke into my house."

He nodded.

"So I may be involved in some way that I don't understand, or it may have to do with my father. He's gotten some people angry recently." She stopped, sighed. "I just wish Alex had a little more faith in me, that he wouldn't jump to incriminating conclusions."

Cassidy shifted in his seat. After several moments of silence, he said, "Alex has been through a rough time lately. It hasn't exactly reinforced his faith in human nature."

The statement was startling—for more than one reason. Somehow she'd assumed that Alex Shane had made it. Or put another way, that he had everything he wanted out of life. Apparently it wasn't true. "When you say a rough time, you're not just talking about his getting arrested. You mean before that?" she pressed.

He sighed. "Probably I shouldn't have said anything."

"Yes, but you did say something. Now you have to explain. Please. I care about him," she said, admitting her feelings for the first time. "I want to understand him better."

Dan's gaze turned inward, then he finally said, "He wouldn't like to know I was talking about his personal business."

"Please. I need to know. He's been so closed up, so cautious. I need to understand why," she pressed, feeling her own edge of desperation. She wasn't usually a pushy person, but she ached to know what had happened to Alex Shane. And maybe her emotions showed on her face.

Dan knit his fingers together. "He caught his wife with another man."

She sucked in a startled breath. Then asked, "He's married?"

"He's divorced now. I think he accepted the assignment down here in St. Stephens partly to get away from the bad memories."

She absorbed that information, thinking it went a long way toward explaining where Alex was coming from.

Dan had said that Alex had lost his faith in human nature. Probably that applied most directly to the female portion of the population.

She mulled that over, watching Dan watch her.

"That must have been pretty rough for him," she murmured.

"Yeah. And now that I've spilled the beans, you probably don't want to let him know. I'm guessing it would be better for him to tell you about it himself—if he tells you at all."

"Right."

"So maybe I haven't done you any favors."

"We'll see," was all she could answer.

Chapter Eight

There were advantages and disadvantages to knowing how the system worked. Alex knew that prisoners being held on felony charges had to be arraigned within forty-eight hours. And he expected to be formally charged because Dan Cassidy, who had stayed in town since first coming down from Baltimore, had told him that the police didn't have any other suspects.

He'd digested that information, along with the facts of life in the county lockup. As a law enforcement officer, he'd known on an intellectual level that jail was dehumanizing. He hadn't realized just how dehumanizing until he'd lived through the experience for two days—being told what to wear, when to get up, when to go to bed and when he could shower.

If he'd shown any sign of weakness, the other prisoners might have made things even worse for him. But he projected a tough-guy exterior that said, "Mess with me, and you'll be damn sorry." The hard-assed act had been as much for himself as for the men locked up with him. He had to stay tight and numb to keep some hold on sanity. Had to function at a minimal level or start acting out his anger and despair.

But it was hard to maintain that icy exterior when he

was brought in a van with other prisoners to the Talbot County Courthouse.

His most fervent hope was that he didn't run into anyone he knew—especially Sara Delaney—not when his hands were shackled and he was wearing a bright orange prison jumpsuit like the other men being transported from the jail.

He felt slightly sick as he waited in a holding cell in the basement of the courthouse. Then a guard called his name, and he was brought upstairs to Judge Raymond Tinker's courtroom.

Dan, who was looking remarkably chipper in a gray suit, off-white shirt and red tie, told him not to worry.

Right.

His pulse was pounding so loudly in his ears that he could barely hear what his attorney was saying.

He tried to tell himself that this was just a formality, but the reality of being charged with murder felt like heavy-metal netting shrouding his body, cutting off his breath.

He heard his name called. Saw Dan respond, then ask to approach the bench.

Now what? He wanted the inevitable over as soon as possible.

When the state's attorney had joined Dan, he handed both the prosecutor and the judge a sheaf of papers.

Both looked them over as Dan waited.

Then the judge raised his head toward Alex. "I have been handed evidence on your case confirming that your weapon was not the one used in the shooting of Emmett Bandy. In addition, tests confirm that your weapon was not fired and that there was no powder residue on your hands. With no evidence to proceed against you, the case is dropped, and you are free to go."

Alex stared at him, hardly able to believe the words. He'd never heard of anything similar happening at an arraignment. He'd never heard of tests being conducted with such efficiency. Dazed, he watched as a deputy removed his handcuffs.

He became aware that Dan was beside him, leading him out of the courtroom.

"How did you manage that?" Alex asked, still stunned. Still unable to believe what he'd just seen with his own eyes and heard with his own ears. "Everybody wants his tests expedited. Nobody gets this kind of express service."

"Randolph Security has helped wrap up a lot of cases in Maryland. Let's just say that Cam Randolph had the clout to speed things up."

"Yeah, well, let's just say I owe you one. You and Cam."

"I was only doing my job. I was hired to take care of legal business for Randolph because I know the ropes in the criminal justice system."

"I'll attest to that. I've never seen anything like what happened in court today."

Dan cleared his throat. "It wasn't just my doing. Clark Hempstead went to bat for you, too."

On hearing that piece of information, Alex could only goggle at his friend. "Hempstead? When he arrested me at Bandy's, he looked like he was ready to lock me up and throw away the key."

"Well, I had a talk with him yesterday. His first reaction was disappointment that you'd gotten yourself into trouble. Given some time to think about it, he realized that you were telling him the truth."

Alex could only shake his head, still trying to absorb the knowledge that he was a free man.

"I brought you some clothes," Dan said. "You can change in the men's room. Then maybe you'd like to come to my motel and take a shower before you go home. I'm only five minutes from here.''

''Yeah,'' Alex agreed. He had been in custody less than forty-eight hours, but the rancid smell of the jailhouse was in his pores.

He changed quickly into slacks and a Polo shirt. After balling up the prison jumpsuit, he handed it to the deputy who had escorted him upstairs. When he and Dan started down the hall, he found Hempstead standing by the door to the parking lot.

Alex stopped dead, his throat going dry.

The chief cleared his throat. ''I, uh, jumped to some conclusions the other morning.''

Alex nodded. ''I understand why.''

''You were a difficult teenager. I was proud of the way you turned out as an adult. I guess I liked to think I had something to do with it.''

''You did.''

''Well, when I saw you standing over Emmett with a gun in your hand, I guess I flashed back on the way it was—the way it could have been.''

''You were doing your job when you arrested me.''

''Yes, but I was angry and disappointed, and I wasn't listening to you. I'm sorry about that.''

''I'm sorry I didn't get the hell out of Bandy's office the moment I found him. I should have known it was a setup.''

''How?''

''Because nothing about this case adds up. Something's going on that I haven't figured out yet.''

''Yeah.''

''So maybe the two of us can trade information later,'' Alex said, extending his hand toward the chief.

Hempstead clasped his hand, and they shook. Then both stood up straighter, looking relieved.

"We'll talk when I get myself together," Alex said.

"When you're ready."

Alex turned and opened the door to the parking lot and immediately regretted the action.

Word had spread quickly about the startling turn of events in Judge Tinker's courtroom, and a crowd of reporters was waiting for the former prisoner.

"Mr. Shane, are you going to sue the state police for false arrest?" a woman asked, thrusting a microphone at him.

"The police were just doing their job. I'm just glad it was quickly proven that the case against me was nonexistent."

"How was the ballistics testing expedited so quickly?"

"You'll have to ask the state police about that."

"How do you feel now?"

"Relieved. And anxious to put this behind me."

"You're investigating the disappearance of Lee Tillman?"

Alex swore under his breath. Who the hell had clued this pack of jackals in about Tillman? Aloud he said, "I don't know that he's disappeared. He's on vacation."

"Mr. Shane—"

He pulled himself together to deliver a nice little sound bite. "I have faith in the American justice system. I know I would have eventually been cleared of all charges. I'm just glad it happened sooner than later. That's all I have to say."

Dan was beside him as he walked rapidly down the steps, scanning the crowd as he went.

A familiar figure on the grass strip at the edge of the parking lot swam into his vision, and his steps faltered.

Standing with his arms folded across his chest was his brother.

Billy gave him a sardonic smile as if to say, "You think you're better than I am. You joined the clean team. But look what's happened to you."

He saw Dan follow his gaze.

"Who's that creep?" his friend asked.

"My ex-con brother."

"Sorry."

"No need to apologize. If they'd caught him standing over a body with a gun in his hand, it would be a good bet that he'd done the deed." He looked away from the man whose failure was somehow his own. "Come on. Let's get out of here."

While Alex showered, washed his hair and shaved, Dan bought breakfast. Biscuits with gravy, ham and eggs—indulgences that Alex didn't usually allow himself to enjoy. This morning he wolfed them down, along with several cups of coffee laced with half and half.

Once more he thanked his friend for everything he'd done, then realized that he wasn't going anywhere on his own without his vehicle and driver's license. So Dan ran him over to the state police barracks to retrieve his personal property, including his shoulder holster and SUV. The gun he'd brought along that night was still at the crime lab.

They had additional business to discuss, so Dan followed him home. As he approached his driveway, he saw a car blocking the entrance. Alex tensed, suddenly very sorry that he was unarmed.

The door slammed open, and a man wearing a rumpled gray suit jumped out. "Mr. Shane! Mr. Shane!"

Alex recognized the guy. He was a reporter who had

shown up in Baltimore a couple of times during high-profile cases.

Alex rolled down his window. "Get the hell out of here."

"Mr. Shane, I'm from the *National Tattler*. We're willing to pay for your story of false arrest."

"Well, I'm not willing to talk. And if you're still here in fifteen minutes, I'll shoot you."

The guy's eyes narrowed. Probably in his line of work, he'd heard worse threats. But he climbed back into his car and drove away.

"How many more of those are there going to be?" Alex wondered aloud as he and Dan pulled up in front of the house and climbed out of their vehicles.

"Shoot one, and it will ease off real quick," Dan answered.

"Yeah, right."

Alex unlocked the front door, and they both went inside. Alex's first stop was his office.

Lying on the desk beside the answering machine was his Glock and a folded note.

Quickly he opened it.

Alex, thank you for everything. I've gone to my dad's, like you suggested.

"From Sara?" Dan asked.

"Yeah," he answered, remembering that he'd told Dan he wasn't sure how she was involved in the Tillman case.

"She was here when I stopped by a couple of days ago."

"You spoke to her?"

"I came over to tell her what we were doing to get you out of jail. She seemed like a nice woman," Dan said.

"So did Cindy," Alex retorted, wanting to tell Cassidy to mind his own business when it came to his personal life. But it didn't seem like the thing to do, considering what the man had just done for him. Instead, he unlocked the door and stepped out onto the deck where he stood looking across at the creek.

After a moment, Dan followed him outside.

"Sorry about the outburst. I'm not in real good shape," Alex said.

"That's understandable."

For several moments, the only sound was Dan kicking at a place where a board was splintered. "I know you don't want my advice. So I won't give you any. I'll just say that you weren't around when I met my wife, Sabrina." He laughed. "She was a suspect in a murder case, and I was the state's attorney trying to get the goods on her. But we'd had problems before that." Dan laughed again. "Actually, we had a pretty long history of conflict."

Alex stared at him. "You're kidding."

"It was a kind of trial by fire, but we worked things out."

Not sure what to say, Alex simply stood there.

"Don't make assumptions about Sara."

"I saw her sneaking into Tillman's office! Then somebody went after her. I know she's tied in to this somehow."

"Just keep an open mind. Don't let a marriage that turned bad make it impossible to trust another relationship."

"We don't *have* a relationship!"

"Well, I'd say she cares about you."

"How do you know?" Alex demanded.

"Maybe it would be better if you figured that out for

yourself. Besides, I've been away from my wife for a couple of days, and I'm anticipating the reunion.''

Instantly, Alex felt guilty. Dan had been down here in St. Stephens working his ass off to get him out of jail, and now he was detaining him with questions he had no business asking.

"You'd better make tracks for Baltimore, then," he said. "And thank you again—for everything."

"No problem."

Alex expected his friend to leave immediately, but he remained where he was, shifting his weight slightly from one foot to the other, giving the impression that he wanted to say something more. Something that Alex wasn't going to like hearing.

"You might as well spit it out," he said, struggling to keep his voice mild.

Dan sighed. "You had a pretty bad time over the past couple of days. I didn't want to say anything while you were in custody, but…"

"But what?" Alex snapped.

"But keeping that meeting with Bandy wasn't the smartest thing you ever did."

"Thanks!"

"Alex, I don't like to see you being reckless."

"I'm not."

Dan shrugged. "Just think about it, will you?"

Alex shoved his hands into his pockets. "So, are you going to write up a recommendation that Randolph Security take me off the case?" he asked.

"Of course not."

"Thanks for that. And thanks for getting me out of the slammer."

"Alex, take care of yourself."

"I will," he said automatically.

Dan walked back to his car. Alex turned and went into the house. In his office he stared at the flashing red light on the answering machine. Probably nobody had called that he wanted to talk to. But he'd better check the messages—in case Lee had tried to contact him again.

There was no further communication from the evasive Lee Tillman. The bulk of the calls were from reporters wanting an interview. Two were from townspeople who advised him to go back to the other side of the Bay Bridge where he belonged.

Great!

After erasing the tape, he stared at his desk—and at the gun sitting beside his keyboard.

He'd left it for Sara's protection. He didn't know if she had a weapon of her own.

His mind jumped from protecting her to considering the consequences of leaving her alone in his house. She'd been in his office, which meant that she could have gone through his files if she were so inclined. Paper files, because his computer was password protected.

He canceled the negative thoughts and went back to worrying about the trouble she was in. She'd said she was going to her father's. But had she stayed put?

He reached for the phone book, found Reid Delaney's number and dialed. When a man said hello, he asked to speak to Sara.

"Who is this?" The voice turned belligerent.

"Alex Shane."

"The jerk-off private eye who got himself arrested?" Delaney asked, his words not exactly steady. It sounded as if Sara hadn't been lying about the drinking.

Alex sighed. "Can I speak to your daughter?"

"She's not here. And if she was, I wouldn't let you talk to her."

"Thanks." He wasn't sure he believed that Sara wasn't home. On the other hand, he had just confirmed some additional information. The old guy was a hard case.

"What are you doing for her—trying to find her birth parents so she can go back to them and leave me?" Mr. Delaney suddenly demanded.

The quick change of subject had Alex doing a double take. "No."

Delaney snorted. "Sure. Why else would she have hired a P.I.?"

"I'm not working for her. We're friends."

"Sure," the elder Delaney said again.

"She's been interested in finding her birth parents?" Alex asked.

"Don't play dumb with me, sonny. You know damn well she's been up to something in that department."

"News to me."

"She contacted that place in Baltimore. Birth Day, Inc., or whatever you call it."

"Birth Data?" Alex asked, keeping the surprise out of his voice. Birth Data was part of the Light Street Foundation—funded by one of his friends, Travis Stone, and run by his wife, Erin Stone.

"They couldn't do a damn thing for her," Delaney sneered.

The guy was being pretty talkative. Probably that was how liquor affected him. Alex wondered how to direct the conversation.

"Did she have any problems with Lee Tillman?" he asked.

"That bastard!"

"What did Tillman do to you?"

"He was sweet on her."

Alex felt his chest tighten. "How do you know?" he asked.

"He did stuff for her. Got her jobs. Paid her more than she was worth. Lent her the money to buy her house."

"He did?"

"Well, he called it a mortgage. But God knows what she was doing to earn the dough."

Alex winced. His mind was spinning now.

Was Reid Delaney angry enough at Lee Tillman to kill him? That possibility had suddenly become a promising line of investigation.

And what about the other piece of information the man had just imparted? Sara had been trying to locate her birth parents. Suppose when she'd started asking questions, she'd attracted someone's attention? Suppose someone was coming after her because they knew she was the natural daughter of a prominent citizen who didn't want a shameful incident in his or her past revealed?

He remembered talking to Travis and Erin Stone about the adoption ring that had once operated in St. Stephens. Local girls had been sent to a home for unwed mothers and then forced to give up their babies for adoption. The doctor and the lawyer running the place had pocketed big fees. In fact, Travis Stone had been one of those babies.

"Did you get Sara from a mother who lived in the area?" Alex asked the elder Delaney.

"None of your damn business."

He tried another approach. "I guess it's pretty upsetting when the child you raised wants to contact people she never even met, people who didn't want to stay in contact with her."

"You're damn right. And stop trying to pump me for information." The man slammed down the phone, leaving Alex listening to empty air.

He carefully replaced the receiver, now wanting more than ever to speak to Sara. This time he tried her home phone. All he got was the answering machine, and he wasn't sure what to say. He didn't want to leave a message about the adoption search, since it was probably a sensitive subject with her. Nor did he know what to say about himself, either.

"Hi. I'm out of jail. Let's get together."

Trying to ignore his feeling of frustration, he pulled out his file on Sara and found her birthday. Then he looked up the Birth Data number in his Rolodex.

When he asked for Erin Stone, he was put through quickly.

"Alex," she said. "I'm so glad everything worked out for you."

"Yeah. Thanks," he answered, thinking that probably everybody he knew was talking about how he'd gotten arrested for murder. Probably there were guys at Randolph who thought he'd been stupid getting caught in the wrong place at the wrong time.

That was another topic he didn't want to discuss.

"I was hoping you could help me with the case I'm working on."

"If I can."

"You remember we talked about an adoption ring that operated in St. Stephens twenty-five to forty years ago?"

"Yes."

"Well, there's a young woman mixed up in the case I'm working on."

"The Lee Tillman case?"

"Yes," he acknowledged, thinking that he might as well write an editorial about it for the *Baltimore Sun*. "I've found out that she consulted you."

"Alex, our records are confidential."

"I know that, and I wasn't going to ask you about her, specifically. But I was thinking about when you and Travis exposed that adoption scam. Could you tell me if there was a baby girl put up for adoption through the service in late July 1974?"

"Just a moment."

He waited for several minutes. Then Erin came on the line again. "There are no records of a girl being born to any of the mothers from Ashwood, the estate where the unwed mothers lived."

Something about the tone of her voice made him ask, "But?"

"But, um…"

"Erin!"

"Okay. I don't have any details. But I see that there's a five-thousand-dollar payment to William DeGeorge, the lawyer who arranged the adoptions."

"Five thousand dollars," he repeated.

"That's well below his usual fee."

"Do you know who paid him?"

"Alex, I'm skirting the confidentiality rules now. If I had that information, I couldn't give it to you," she said quickly.

An idea hit him, and he asked, "Did fathers ever arrange for adoptions?"

"I can't give out that information."

He cleared his throat. "I appreciate what you could tell me."

"It wasn't much. Take care, Alex."

"I will."

He hung up, musing over the conversation and wondering if he was going to end up breaking into the office of Birth Data, Inc. Or maybe there was another approach he could take. Like perhaps having another chat with Sara's father.

There was an additional piece of business he should take care of. Getting directory information. He called the hotel in Nova Scotia where Lee was supposed to be headed. He hadn't arrived, but Alex did find out that he wasn't due for another two days. He should check Lee's route, too, seeing if he'd registered in any hotels along the way. He turned that job over to Randolph Security, then leaned back in his chair, bonetired. Two sleepless nights in prison suddenly hit him like a hard right to the jaw, and he knew if he didn't get some quality time in the sack, he wouldn't be able to function. So he turned off the phone and staggered into the bedroom where he threw off his clothing and crawled under the covers.

Some time later, the ringing phone woke him up.

Hadn't he turned off the damn phone? Confused, he wondered if he was having auditory hallucinations. Then he realized it was the cell phone in his pants pocket.

He found where he'd thrown the pants and pulled out the instrument, glancing at the window. Dim light filtered through the blinds, informing him he'd slept the clock around.

Shaking his head, he slid his gaze back to the numbers on the display and blinked when he recognized them. Sara.

When he pressed the receive button on the phone, her voice leaped through the receiver.

"Alex, thank God!" she gasped. "I thought…I thought you weren't going to be there."

"Sara, what's wrong?"

Her voice rose an octave. "Dad and I had a fight. So I left."

"I told you—"

She cut him off before he could finish. "Two of those

guys were waiting for me when I got home. I—I jumped in my car and drove away. But they're following me. What should I do?''

"Keep moving. I'll get to you as soon as I can."

"Okay."

"And keep the line open, even if we're not talking!"

"Yes," she answered, a sob of relief in her voice.

It flashed into his mind that he'd gotten into a hell of a lot of trouble a couple of days ago because he'd been carrying a weapon. But there was no question of leaving his piece home now. If the two guys who were after Sara were armed, then going up against them bare was suicidal. Besides, he had a permit to carry.

So he shoved the Glock into his belt. Then he grabbed a baseball cap and pulled it down over his eyes. Still, when he stepped out of the house, a flashbulb went off in his face.

"Get the hell off my property," he snapped at the persistent guy.

As he stalked toward the man with the camera, the reporter turned and ran.

"Alex?" Sara's voice came over the phone.

"It's okay. Another member of the fourth estate coming after me." Jumping in his SUV, he started the engine. "Where are you?"

"On the Old River Road."

"They're following you in a truck?"

"Yes."

"What color?"

"Green."

"Stay on the highway. I'll be there as quickly as I can."

As he roared to the end of the driveway, he thanked Providence that nobody else was lying in wait for him.

"Are these the same guys that have been showing up?" he asked Sara.

"I can't tell."

"Baseball caps?"

"Yes." Her voice rose in panic. "Alex, they keep coming up next to me, trying to push me onto the shoulder."

He swore as he pressed down on the accelerator. "How far are you from town?"

"I'm near the park."

"What park?"

He heard her gulp. "Muncaster Park, where you and I…you know."

Yeah, he did know. His memories of that incident were pretty vivid. But up until now, she hadn't given him any indication that she remembered him.

He might have pursued that startling piece of information if she hadn't been in the middle of a damn mess. He wanted to yell at her, tell her again that going back to her house had been a bad idea. But there was no point in cursing her out now.

Now he had to get to her—before the guys who were trying to hurt her.

He wanted to speed down the highway at eighty miles an hour, but he was stuck behind a little old geezer going forty-five. A truck was coming in the other direction, but Alex chanced a pass, whipping back into his lane seconds before the big vehicle sped past, the driver honking his horn for all he was worth.

With part of his mind he was thinking that it wouldn't be a dumb idea to call the cops for backup. But he couldn't do it without breaking the connection with Sara, and he needed to keep on top of what was going on. That was what he told himself. But he knew he had another reason for doing this his way. It was difficult to picture the cops rushing to his aid after his recent experiences with them.

And there was another factor, too. Sara had called *him*, when she could have called the law.

He had just made another dangerous pass, when her gasp on the other end of the line riveted his attention.

"What's happening?"

"They're forcing me off the road again. This time...I can't stay on the pavement."

"How close are you to the park?"

"A quarter of a mile."

"Turn in to the entrance."

"But I'll be trapped."

"Do it! I'll get to you," he promised, praying that it was true, because if he couldn't get there in time, he'd made her situation worse.

He heard tires squealing, then the crunch of gravel.

He pictured the access road. At the end of the road a right fork led to a riverside drive, the left fork led to pavement that wound into the woods.

"Turn right as soon as you can."

"Along the river?"

"Yeah."

As he passed the sign announcing the park, he took the turn on two tires. Straightening out, he sped down the access road.

"I'm almost there," he panted, feeling as if he was running a race.

He heard Sara make a small, choked sound.

"What?"

"They're pushing me toward the water."

"Hang on."

"I'm on the sand. Oh God, the pier's ahead of me. I'm going to hit it."

He heard brakes squealing.

"Sara! Sara! "

She didn't answer. "Talk to me, Sara," he shouted.

There were several moments of silence, during which all he could hear was the blood roaring in his ears. He kept shouting her name, kept racing along the road at dangerous speed, taking the fork she had taken, thinking that if he crashed he wasn't going to do her much good. But he couldn't make himself slow down.

The gray water came into view, and the long stretch of sand along the shoreline. Ahead of him he saw the pier and two vehicles.

What had happened was immediately apparent. The driver of the other car had been focused on Sara. When she'd stopped short, he'd kept going and barely missed the pilings.

As he watched, the doors of the green truck flew open. Two guys got out and started heading back toward Sara's car.

Even at this distance, he recognized one of them, and the hairs on the back of his neck stood on end.

It was his brother, Billy.

He growled a curse, his voice filling the inside of the truck as he sped the last hundred yards to the scene and braked to a stop.

The two men were on Sara's side of the car, facing her, so neither one of them was aware that company had arrived.

Sara's door must be locked, thank God. He could hear the other guy shouting at her to open up. When she didn't comply, he pulled a handgun from the waistband of his pants, raised it over his head and brought the butt crashing down against her window.

Alex tossed the cell phone on the seat beside him, then

drew his own gun as he leaped from the SUV. "Step away from the car, and leave the lady alone," he ordered.

Billy and the hothead both whirled to face him, surprise and anger warring on their faces. The latter had been caught holding his gun by the wrong end, since he'd been using it as a club.

"Drop your weapons and step away from the car," Alex said.

Billy cocked his head to one side, studying him. "What are you going to do, shoot your own brother?"

"If I have to."

Billy shrugged, but his tone was belligerent as he said, "You got yourself a good lawyer, so you lucked out at the courthouse. You're going to be back in the slammer if you shoot someone now. So you'd be smart to back off."

"I wouldn't test that theory if I were you," Alex answered, his voice firm and flat.

Billy's jaw jutted out the way it had when they were kids, squabbling. His eyes narrowed. He wasn't holding a weapon, but the bulge under his shirt was pretty suggestive.

For a long moment, Alex didn't know which way it was going to go.

Chapter Nine

Alex saw Sara staring through the network of cracks where the gun butt had crashed against the window. It was safety glass so it hadn't shattered. But another blow might be enough to cave it in.

She looked scared, but defiant, as if she was going to give the guy some grief if he came in there to get her.

Well, he wasn't going to let that happen.

"Drop your weapon and step away from the car," he repeated, wondering if the hothead was stupid enough to try repositioning the gun before shooting at an armed man.

To his vast relief the guy must have calculated his odds and decided that his chances weren't good. Slowly he stepped away from Sara's car. When the gun hit the ground, Alex let out the breath that had been frozen in his lungs.

"You too, Billy," he ordered.

His brother gave him a scathing look as he reached under his shirt, slowly pulled out an automatic and dropped it beside the one already on the sand.

"Walk to the river," Alex said.

"What are you going to do?"

"The river!" he snapped.

After several moments' hesitation, they looked at each other and started for the water. Billy did the same.

"Wade in."

The two men stepped cautiously as the water lapped at their ankles and then their knees.

"Keep going. Move it."

They followed orders, wading farther and farther into the gray river until the waves swallowed their thighs, then their waists.

Alex turned his head and motioned to Sara. She eased the door of her car open, then crossed to him.

"Get into my truck," he said quietly. "I'll be there in a minute."

He expected her to do what he told her to do. Instead, she coolly picked up a kitchen knife that must have been on the seat beside her. She hadn't exactly mentioned that detail.

As he watched, she marched toward the green truck, bent and ripped at the side of the left front tire, slashing through the wall. When the air began to leak out, she moved to the rear of the vehicle and repeated the process.

"Two is enough," he called out. "They're probably not carrying around two spare tires."

"Okay."

At the sound of Alex's voice, his brother's partner half turned. "Hey, what the hell are you doing to my tires?" he shouted.

"Let's get out of here," Alex told Sara.

They got into the SUV and as he made a quick U-turn, he saw the two men in the water struggling awkwardly toward the shore.

He drove back the way he'd come, toward the fork where the two roads branched off.

When he was out of sight of the river, he turned to Sara. She was huddled in her seat, shivering.

He glanced in the rearview mirror. The road behind them was clear. He didn't expect Billy and his friend to get their vehicle going any time soon. And Sara's car was too new to be hot-wired. They might have a cell phone, however, to call for reinforcements. If they did, Alex didn't want to be anywhere in the vicinity.

He exited the park, drove down the highway at a moderately fast pace and took a road that led to a development of large homes built along a golf course.

Pulling to the shoulder under the overhanging branches of some trees, he cut the engine and swung toward Sara.

"Are you okay?"

"Yes. Thank God you came."

"Thank God you kept your head," he answered, then asked the question that had been in his mind earlier. "Why didn't you call the cops? Were you still worried about your dad?"

Her eyes widened. "I—I didn't think about the cops. I thought about you. Just you," she added in a whisper. "You talked me through the terror, but I dropped my phone when I slammed on the brakes."

"So that's why I couldn't get you!"

"I could hear you shouting at me. You were still there."

"Well, you were the one who held them off long enough for me to get to you. And then you slashed the hell out of their tires. Where did you get the knife?"

"Your kitchen. I left your house with it."

He laughed. So it was *his* kitchen knife. He sobered as he reached for her, pulled her toward him, and she came into his arms with a small sound.

"Why did you go home?" he demanded.

"I was at my dad's. He let it slip that you'd called, and

he hadn't let me talk to you. I was so angry with him that I had to get out of there.'' In response to his strangled exclamation, she went on quickly, ''You don't have to tell me again. Going home was a bad idea. But I wasn't planning to stay there. A friend of mine is away in Europe and I have the key to her condo so I can water her plants. I was going there as soon as I picked up some clean clothes.''

Mollified, he nodded.

''I was worried about you, too,'' she murmured. ''I mean, after you called me from the state police.''

''I'm back safe and sound.''

''Thank God for that. I knew you didn't do it.''

''How?''

''I just knew!''

There was an unaccustomed clarity to the scene. The sunlight beyond the trees, the dappled shade where the truck was parked, the mixture of relief and joy on Sara's face as she looked up at him.

He saw her eyes drift shut just as his lips met hers.

He felt a melting sensation, as though his mouth was flowing against hers, his body melding to hers, absorbing the feel of her, the taste, the wonderful scent of her.

The events of the past few days swirled in his head. He'd been in custody less than forty-eight hours, but he felt as if he'd been away from her for an eternity. And then their first contact had been a cry for help.

Thank God she'd had a cell phone. Thank God he'd been out of jail and able to come when she called. Thank God she was in his arms now—and that she seemed as eager for his kisses as he was to give them.

He was lost in the reality of her. Of them. It flitted through his mind that this was meant to be all along. And the years without her had only been an unfortunate interruption.

She moaned into his mouth.

There were no words to express the depth and breadth of his emotions. All he could do was shut out the world and move his mouth over hers, move his hands over her back, into her hair.

"Alex." His name sighed out of her like a prayer of thanks.

"I'm here. Right here," he answered, easing her lips apart so that he could taste her more fully.

He sipped from her, nibbled, devoured, until he was shaking with the strength of his response. He wanted to slip his hands under her shirt and splay them against the warm skin of her back. He wanted to slide them around and cup her breasts, tease her nipples. But he was already in danger of taking this too far out here on a public road, with the bad guys somewhere behind them.

When he dragged his mouth away from hers, she made a sharp sound of protest.

"Not here," he whispered.

She blinked, looked around as though she'd just remembered where they were.

Drawing away from him, she smoothed her hair. He wondered if she regretted melting into his arms. He wondered what she would say if he brought up the subject of the park. Not a few minutes ago. But eleven years ago.

They had personal business to discuss. But none of it was as urgent as Billy and his partners.

"We have to talk, but this isn't a good place. Not when those guys could call their buddies."

"Where should we go?"

"Your house isn't safe." He thought about the recent

incidents with the press. "Neither is mine, because I can't step out the door without tripping over a reporter."

"Oh Lord, Alex, I'm sorry."

He ran a hand through his hair, thinking.

"My friend Wendy's apartment," she said. "We can go there."

"Where does she live?"

"In one of those new condos down by the water."

He considered the suggestion, not loving the location. It was smack in the middle of town, which meant too many people were around. "How far is the walk from the car to the door?"

"She's right on the parking lot."

So they could get inside quickly. "Okay."

He drove back into St. Stephens, paying as much attention to the rearview mirror as the road ahead of him.

"Which apartment?" he asked as he approached the condos.

"Her number is 752. It's around back."

He followed her directions, still watching the other traffic and making sure that nobody was paying them any particular attention. Satisfied, he pulled into a space a couple of dozen feet from the building's entrance.

Nobody was walking in the immediate area when he stepped quickly out of the SUV and escorted Sara into the stairwell. He was glad to see the apartment was on the second floor. At least the bad guys wouldn't be coming in the sliding glass door.

She inserted the key in the lock, and they stepped into a large, comfortable-looking room. An overstuffed plum-colored velvet sofa and chairs were set off by antique cabinet pieces—a sideboard, an armoire. Tall plants were grouped near a sliding glass door that led to a narrow balcony.

But the thing he noticed most was that he was now alone with Sara.

She set down her purse on one of the chairs. When she turned back to him, he could feel the sudden tension radiating from her and feel his own tension. "Maybe this isn't such a good idea," he said quickly.

She didn't quite meet his eyes as she repeated what he'd pointed out earlier. "This is probably the best place to talk."

Talk. He'd brought her here to talk, he reminded himself as he wiped his suddenly damp palms against his pants legs.

When he saw her follow the motion, he made an effort to sound coherent. "You said before that you were worried about your dad, so you didn't want to get the police involved. I think we'd both be better off if we got what happened with those guys on record."

He saw her swallow. "Okay."

Just like that, she agreed.

He pulled out the cell phone he'd shoved into his pocket and turned it in his hand. "Before I call, did you recognize either of those guys?"

"They're some of the men I told you about. The ones who have been following me around. And..."

"And what?" he asked sharply.

"I saw one of them on television in the crowd of people outside Bandy's office after you were arrested. I thought he looked like you. Is he...related?"

He sighed out a breath, and she tipped her head toward him.

"Remember I told you about my family history, that my brother never left town except when he was in prison. And you thought it wasn't relevant."

"That was him?" she said, not sounding surprised.

"Yes."

"I'm so sorry," she breathed. "I mean…"

"It's okay. I know what you mean." He clenched and unclenched his fists. "At least I know that if it's been going on for a while, he can't be doing it to get back at me."

"Get back at you? What does he have against you?"

"I turned my life around. He couldn't. That's made him…hostile." Wanting to change the subject before she asked any more questions, he said, "Maybe Hempstead has some ideas. But maybe we shouldn't go down to the police station. Maybe it would be better if we see if he can meet us somewhere."

"Why?"

"Two reasons. You said Billy and his friends were at your house. If they're expecting you to show up downtown, they might try to head you off. And maybe it's better if they think I'm afraid to call the police after just getting out of the slammer."

She answered with a tight nod, then said, "Don't call the chief yet."

"Why not?"

She gave him a questioning look. "Did you just bring me here to talk?"

Had he?

Maybe she saw the answer in his eyes, because she took a step toward him. "Alex," she breathed, crossing the distance between them and reaching for him.

He reached at the same time, folding her close.

She let out a small sigh as she laid her head against his shoulder.

He should step away from her, but he couldn't make his muscles follow through on the thought.

"Alex, when I heard you'd been arrested, I was so worried. And guilty."

"Guilty?" he asked, his voice raspy. "What did *you* do?"

"Nothing to get you in trouble," she said quickly. "It's more like I started thinking about the things that have happened between us. Each meeting, and how we keep rubbing each other the wrong way. And I didn't want it to be like that. So I decided that when you got out, I'd let you know how I was really feeling."

"How?"

She lifted her head, brought her mouth to his, a small sound of need rising in her throat. He had wanted this, dreamed about it as he lay on the hard bunk in the dank confines of his jail cell because he needed to hold on to something good. Sara.

"Alex?" she murmured against his mouth.

In response he angled his head to claim more complete possession of her, his tongue taking wicked advantage of her parted lips.

She tasted like a field of flowers spread across a sunlit landscape. And she said his name again, her hands sweeping across his shoulders, then sliding upward to cup the back of his head.

But there was no need to hold him in place. Not when a forest fire of wanting had kindled itself between them— scorching his skin, burning a path through his blood.

He couldn't get enough of her. He needed to taste, to touch. His mouth never leaving hers, he slid his hands under her shirt, his fingers splaying across the soft skin of her back.

Finding the catch of her bra, he slipped it open, then pushed it out of the way as he brought his hands around to her front, lifting and cupping her breasts.

The sounds of pleasure she made were like sparks striking dry kindling. His fingers found the hardened tips of her breasts, circled them, crested over them.

When he finally lifted his mouth from hers, they were both out of breath.

There must be a bedroom down the hall, and he pictured himself sweeping her into his arms and carrying her there.

But somewhere in his fevered brain, reason surfaced. He managed to say, "We can't."

"Why not?"

"Because I'm not prepared to protect you."

She lifted her eyes toward his. "You're still being a gentleman."

"Still?"

He saw her close her eyes for just a moment before blinking them open again. "Like in the back seat of that car, when you could have taken my virginity."

As his brain processed her words, he went absolutely still.

Her eyes never left his. "Maybe it's good I blurted it out awhile ago. We had to talk about it eventually. Alex, it's something I've thought about over the years. It's one of my best memories. And that's the God's honest truth."

For him, too.

"I've thought about how good it was with you. And neither one of us ever took our clothes off."

His mouth had gone dry. "But you didn't say anything when we saw each other again," he managed to tell her.

She gave a small, shaky laugh. "I couldn't. What was I supposed to say? Hey, aren't you the guy who could have nailed me at that beer party?"

He gave a tight nod, seeing it from her point of view.

"I was embarrassed. It was easier to hope you didn't remember me."

"Not a chance."

"You didn't mention it either."

"Maybe I was still being a gentleman." That was part of it, certainly. He wasn't going to add the rest—that he'd suspected her motives for coming into Lee Tillman's office.

She was speaking again. "Right. A gentleman. You could have done anything you wanted with me that night. But you stopped. Why did you stop?"

"You were sweet and innocent, and I didn't want to take advantage of you."

"I'm not so sweet and innocent now. I mean—" She broke off the sentence, flushed. "Well, I'm not the most experienced woman you ever met. But I'm experienced enough to know what I want." She held his gaze, sure and steady. "I told you I was thinking about what might happen when you got out of jail. So I dropped by the drugstore. I mean, I figured you wouldn't be prepared so I'd better be."

"The drugstore where all the locals hang out?"

She flushed again. "No. I drove to Cambridge. I didn't want my personal business spread all over town."

He laughed, feeling almost light-headed as he took her hand and led her down the hall.

The bedroom was waiting for them. Stepping inside, he set his gun on the dresser, then turned back to Sara and gathered her to him.

"You're shaking," he murmured. "Are you sure this is what you want?"

"You're shaking, too."

"Yeah."

Whatever else he might have said turned into a long sigh of pleasure as she slipped her hands under his shirt and stroked them in slow sweeps across his back.

In his mind he had played out this scene many times over the years since that night in the car. She was the one girl he'd let get away. He'd known back then that turning her loose was the right thing to do. But it hadn't stopped him from wondering what if?

Now the reality of holding her, touching her, kissing her was better than anything he could have imagined.

He took a step back, pulled the shirt over his head and tossed it onto the chair. Then he began unbuttoning her shirt, removing it along with her bra.

He saw the sudden flash of nerves in her eyes and knew that despite her earlier boldness, she wasn't all that conversant with men and bedrooms. Somewhere in his mind he thought he should stop. But he had given up chivalry. Pulling her into his arms, he groaned at the soft pressure of her breasts against his chest, craving her on some deep elemental level, the way a thirsty man craves water.

They swayed together, touching, kissing, sighing.

He turned away long enough to pull down the spread and the blanket. She stepped away from him and grabbed her purse, rummaging for her drugstore purchase, which she set on the bedside table, her head bent away from him.

He caught her in his arms again, stroking her, then shucking her shorts and panties down her legs.

"You are so beautiful," he breathed. "If I'd known how beautiful, you never would have gotten off so easy."

"I don't want to get off easy now," she whispered.

"Oh, you won't."

When her hands centered on his belt buckle, he went very still. His arms at his sides, he watched her as she unbuckled the belt, then started on his slacks.

His breath caught as she lowered his zipper, then slid her hand into the opening she'd made, slid beneath the elastic band of his briefs to cup his aching erection.

It took all his strength to say, "Don't. Don't go so fast." But he said it because he wanted this to be good for her, as good as he could make it.

Taking her down to the surface of the bed, he gathered her to him, kissed her softly, tenderly.

When his hands found her breasts, shaping them to his touch, he gloried in her long sigh of pleasure. He followed the caress with his lips, and now he was the one who exclaimed, unable to believe that anything could feel so good in his mouth as the taut flesh of her erect nipples.

One of her hands winnowed through his hair, holding him to her, while the other stroked restlessly over his back and shoulders.

Tender, possessive feelings welled up in him. He knew that he had craved her touch since that long-ago time together. And he knew more—that loving her brought him a fulfillment he'd never felt in his marriage bed.

"Alex, please," she moaned.

He lifted his head, rained small kisses over her face. "Not yet, sweetheart. Not until you're as hot and needy as I am."

"I am—"

He didn't give her a chance to say more. He stopped her words with his lips on her mouth and his hand sliding into the soft feminine folds of her.

She was slick and ready for him, her hips moving restlessly as he brought her up to the level where he wanted her.

She clutched his shoulders, tried to lever him on top of her. But he stayed where he was, absorbed by the feel of her, by the sounds she was making for him.

"Alex, this time I want you inside me when I come," she gasped out.

He wanted that, too. Had wanted it for a thousand years.

"Yes," he managed to say, then reached for the packet she'd set on the bedside table.

When he was ready for her, he turned back, gave her a long, lingering kiss, then moved over her, stroking the hard shaft of his erection against her before cupping her hips, lifting her as he drove forward, his body staking its claim on hers.

She called his name as he began to move within her, dug her nails into his shoulders as he quickened the pace.

When his hand slipped between them to stroke her, he felt her inner muscles contract around him.

He couldn't hold back a deep growl of satisfaction as she came undone for him, triggering his own soul-shattering explosion of pleasure.

Chapter Ten

Sara lay cradled in Alex's arms, listening to the sound of his breathing, feeling his heart beating.

She wanted to tell him that he'd just fulfilled one of her most powerful fantasies—making love with Alex Shane. And it had been as good as she'd imagined. Better, actually.

In the years since their one brief encounter, she'd never gotten over him. Never secretly given up the hope that he would somehow come back into her life. "Alex?"

"Um."

"Thank you."

His hand stroked over her arm, but he said nothing more. She wanted to ask if it had been as wonderful for him as it had been for her, but the words stayed locked in her throat. Something about the way he was holding her warned her that this wasn't the time to ask intimate questions.

He confirmed the suspicion by rolling to his back, although he didn't move away from her.

"Are you all right?" she asked.

"Yeah."

She should keep her mouth shut, but she heard herself ask, "Are you sorry we made love?"

She saw his Adam's apple bob. "I feel like I was taking advantage of you."

"You weren't. I think I made it pretty clear what I wanted."

"You'd just been attacked. You were shaky and vulnerable."

"And I wanted you. I've wanted you for years," she said. "My feelings didn't just spring from what happened today. Remember what I told you. When I was thinking about your getting out of jail, I was thinking about making love with you."

"Because you felt sorry for me?"

"No. Because I stopped kidding myself about what I wanted from you."

"I'm not in any position to make long-term commitments," he said.

"Did I ask for any?"

"Women aren't always straight with guys about what they want."

Dipping her head, she pressed her face against his shoulder, sure that she'd walked into a trap of her own making. She wanted to tell him about her talk with Dan Cassidy. She wanted to tell him that she understood why he might not feel so comfortable making plans for the future. Plans that included a relationship. But she knew he'd resent her conversation with his lawyer. Maybe he'd more than resent it, he'd be downright angry.

She longed to reassure him that she wasn't going to hurt him or betray him. More than that, she longed to say that his getting arrested and going to jail had been a defining experience for her. It had made her realize how much he meant to her—and how much he could mean, if he didn't throw it all away.

Again, the words stayed locked in her throat.

"We were going to call Hempstead," Alex said.

"Yes."

"Uh, we've got a little time-gap problem. So maybe we should tell him that you were upset and needed some breathing space before you talked to him."

"Okay," she answered, thinking that it was kind of true, if you put the right spin on it.

Alex climbed out of bed and started gathering up his clothing. Without looking at him, she did the same, then disappeared into the bathroom, where she tried to keep her mind in neutral as she dressed.

When she emerged once more, she saw that Alex had not only gotten dressed but also made the bed. Was he being considerate of Wendy, or was he trying to wipe out what had happened in this room? she wondered. But she didn't comment.

"Ready?" he asked.

She nodded, and he dialed the number.

"This is Alex Shane," he said when he'd been put through to the chief's office. "It looks like I'm in trouble again."

She was standing close enough to hear the chief's response.

"In what capacity?" he asked.

"Sara Delaney called me to say two men in a pickup were following her and trying to run her off the road. I advised her to turn into Muncaster Park. They smashed her window with a gun butt, but I persuaded them to leave her alone. While they were wading in the river, Sara slashed their tires. Then I got her out of there."

Instead of straining to hear the chief's responses, she walked to the window and turned to face Alex as he said, "A couple of hours ago."

Then, "Well, she was upset. We've been talking. You

might send a man down to the river side of the park to see the vehicles. And you might want to meet with me and Sara. No, not at the police station. How about at the White Swan,'' he suggested, naming the upscale restaurant that was located in a nearby country club.

Alex hung up and looked at her. ''He'll meet us there in twenty minutes.'' He paused, then said, ''I'm, uh, not going to tell him how I got hooked up with you.''

''What are you planning to say?''

''He knows I was hired to investigate Tillman's associates. Your name came up as his accountant.''

''Okay,'' she said tightly.

''You'd prefer some other scenario?''

''No. That's fine.''

''But you're unhappy about it,'' he pressed.

''I don't like duplicity,'' she said tightly.

''Is that why you forgot to mention that you remembered our previous meeting at the park?''

''You forgot to mention it, too,'' she reminded him softly.

He nodded.

''So was I just another one of your conquests back then?'' she heard herself asking.

He laughed. ''If that's all you'd been, we would have gotten a little further into it, don't you think?''

''So what did it mean to you?'' she asked, when what she really wanted to know was how he felt about their lovemaking a few minutes ago.

''We can't talk about it now. We have to meet Hempstead. Do you want him to look at us and think that there's more going on than we're saying?''

''No.''

''Then focus on the fact that two guys attacked you.''

''All right,'' she agreed, thinking that she'd dug herself

into a hole and she wasn't sure how she was going to climb back out.

After they had gotten back into the car, she watched Alex stash his gun in the glove compartment. Five minutes later, they pulled into the restaurant parking lot.

Again he paused and turned to her.

"What?"

"There's something else you should know. When I called your father, he accused me of helping you look for your birth parents."

"I'm sorry he got off on that track."

"He was also sounding off about Lee Tillman."

"Another one of his favorite themes," she conceded, wondering where this was leading.

"He said Lee loaned you the money to buy your house."

"He loaned me the down payment. We have a regular repayment schedule."

"Why would he loan you that kind of money?" Alex asked, his voice mild but his eyes narrowed.

"I guess he liked me, and he was giving me a helping hand."

"That's all?"

"What are you implying?"

"Nothing."

Still, she felt as if he'd slapped her in the face. "If you're asking do I have a sexual relationship with him, the answer is no!"

"Your father thinks it's true."

"My father's always been a little paranoid. It's gotten worse lately."

"Paranoid enough to get rid of Tillman?"

"No!"

He kept the questions coming. "You're sure about that?"

She took her bottom lip between her teeth. "I don't know," she finally admitted.

"Do you know where he was the morning Lee disappeared?"

"At home, as far as I know."

"But you're not certain."

She shook her head.

"I've got to check him out."

"Uh-huh." She opened her door and stepped out of the SUV, turning quickly away from Alex. She was angry with him—and hurt. He'd made love to her a little while ago, and now he was saying her father was a suspect. Worse, he was asking her if she'd been sleeping with Lee.

The part about her father she could understand, especially since she could imagine the morning's conversation. The part about Lee made her realize how far she was from winning Alex's trust.

If she'd had her own car, she would have climbed into it and sped away. But that wasn't an option. And besides, she knew that she had to talk to the police chief.

Still, she was struggling to hold back tears as she marched up the path toward the restaurant.

Alex caught up with her and guided her around a corner and into a small garden area.

"I'm sorry," he said. "I didn't handle that very well."

She kept her face averted.

"I know you aren't sleeping with Lee," he said. "I shouldn't have made it sound like I believed the accusation."

Still unable to raise her face, she asked, "How do you know?"

"I know from the way you made love with me."

"You mean unpolished?"

"No. I mean warm. Generous and a little nervous. Vulnerable." As he spoke he reached for her and pulled her into his arms. She kept her body stiff, still unable to trust him or herself.

"I don't think you're quite Lee's cup of tea."

"Why not?"

"Let's say I know more about him than you do."

When she simply stood there, he muttered, "Please accept my apology."

"Okay," she answered, for the sake of making peace before they faced the police chief together.

ONCE INSIDE the restaurant, Alex told the hostess they were expecting another guest and asked for a table out of the main traffic pattern. She led them past the large windows overlooking the golf course to a table near the back.

Almost as soon as they'd taken their seats, Hempstead strode up to their square wooden table.

He and the chief had talked at the courthouse and then again on the phone, but the man seemed slightly uncomfortable as he slipped into his chair.

Alex wanted to put him at ease. "I appreciate your meeting us here."

The chief nodded before switching his attention to Sara. "Can you tell me what happened?"

"I guess I have to go back a couple of weeks. I've, uh, been seeing guys following me around."

"What guys?"

Sara repeated the description she'd given Alex.

"The militiamen," Hempstead muttered.

Alex's head jerked toward him. "You mean that nutcase group who've taken over the Fairmont Estate?"

"Yeah."

"My brother was one of the men she's talking about. You're telling me he's joined the People's Militia?"

"Yeah," the chief answered again.

"Why didn't we get to that before?"

"It didn't come up. But I've seen him in town with them."

Alex's mind was racing. The group was occupying the old Fairmont Estate, which was actually the next property over from The Refuge.

"Lee had wanted to buy the estate, but old man Fairmont died before they could clinch the deal."

"Why?"

"More land, maybe more prestige?" Alex opened his hands. "Hell, I can't figure out Lee's motivation. In fact, the more I dig into his disappearance, the less I can read the man. At any rate, it looked like old man Fairmont had been willing to sell. But after he died, the son invited his buddies to join him instead. Billy was apparently one of those buddies. Lee had some friction with those guys. I'd gone out on a boat on the river looking at them. They didn't look like rednecks. They wore black uniforms."

"At home, yeah," the chief said. "And sometimes they wear their soldier gear in town when they want to make a certain impression. But in town I've seen guys I recognize from the compound dressed like they just got off the hay wagon from Way Cross, Georgia. Maybe they thought it would make them fit in with the local yokels."

"Smooth move," Alex muttered, then went on quickly. "If they were watching Lee's place, they would have seen Sara going in and out because she's his accountant. And maybe they started following her to get information on him."

"So you think they're responsible for Lee's disappearance?" Hempstead asked.

"I don't know. Maybe. Has anybody heard from Lee since I got myself out of the loop?"

The chief looked regretful. "No."

"He left an answering machine message for me the same evening I got the call from Bandy asking me to come down to his office. At least I thought it was Lee at the time. The call was several hours before Bandy's."

"Bandy and Tillman had some kind of real estate deal going, didn't they?" Hempstead asked.

Alex considered how to answer. If Lee Tillman was still alive, he'd want Alex to keep his personal business private. But if Lee was dead, then the chief needed as much information as he could give him.

He compromised with, "They'd worked together, yes. But recently it was more a case of Bandy borrowing money from Lee. Then the deal fell through, and Lee wanted his money back."

"So could Lee have threatened him?" Hempstead asked. "What if he was strapped for cash and thought he could scare some out of Bandy?"

"When Bandy called, it sounded that way. Now I'm not so sure anything I was fed in that phone call was true. Like, for example, it wasn't Bandy calling me. It was his killer imitating his voice."

The waitress came to take their orders. Alex opted for more food he hadn't been able to get in prison—a burger with blue cheese and tomatoes, coleslaw, french fries and a side order of onion rings.

While they waited for lunch and then after their order arrived, Hempstead talked Sara through the events of the morning.

As Alex listened to her account, he felt his appetite fading. If she hadn't had a phone with her, if she hadn't gotten through to him, then he didn't know what would have happened to her.

She got up to visit the ladies' room, which gave Alex the perfect opportunity to bring up another matter. "I need to ask you about Reid Delaney," he said. "Sara mentioned he'd gotten into some trouble lately."

"Yeah. D and D."

"When I phoned looking for Sara, he started mouthing off about Lee."

"He's an angry man."

"Angry enough to kill?"

"I haven't seen any evidence of that," the chief said. "And from what you've told me, if Lee is dead, the murderer covered it up pretty good. Delaney would have made a mess of it."

Alex felt relieved at crossing Sara's father off his suspect list. By the time Sara returned to the table, he and the chief were discussing the militiamen again.

"Are you going to press charges?" Hempstead asked Sara.

"Should I? Will it stop them from coming after me again?"

The chief considered her question. "I can't advise you on that."

Alex gave him a direct look. "You and I both know that if you arrest them, Billy and the other guy will be out on bail almost instantly. I think for the moment it's better to let them think they got away with something. Meanwhile, we look for a good reason to shut them down."

"Like what?" Sara asked.

"Like maybe they murdered Lee Tillman. Like maybe they're breaking some other laws out on their estate. Probably weapons violations," Alex answered.

"In the meantime, Ms. Delaney's in danger," Hempstead pointed out. "So are you, for that matter."

"She's in danger whether she presses charges or not," Alex said. "If she makes a stink about it, that might make things worse. They may decide to eliminate the witness against them."

"So what do you suggest?" Hempstead asked.

"She needs a place to stay where they won't find her. And a bodyguard."

SARA SAT THERE looking from one man to the other, listening to them discuss her.

Finally she shoved her way into the conversation. "The bodyguard thing didn't work so well last time."

Alex glared at her. "Yeah, well, next time I won't walk into a trap."

Hempstead shifted in his seat. "Maybe you two should work out the details later."

Alex nodded, picked up an onion ring and took a bite. They had been hot and crisp at the beginning of the meal. Now they were cold and congealed. He pushed his plate away, then asked the waitress to wrap it up.

When they were back in the car, Sara pleated the hem of her shirt. "I don't mean to be ungrateful. But you can't just expect me to go along with your plans."

"You don't have to go along with my plans. You can go visit out-of-state friends until it's safe to come back."

"I have my work! Clients are depending on me. I can't just take off."

"Then we'll go back to plan A. It's not like you have to go to the office. You can work from wherever we're staying, because nothing's changed. Your house isn't safe. And neither is mine now."

She looked down at her lap. She knew she couldn't just

go back to her own house, not after what had happened this morning. Next time they might kill her. But the idea of staying with Alex carried its own threat. She wanted to grab his arm, turn him toward her and ask him where the two of them stood.

First he'd made exquisite love to her. Then he'd accused her of sleeping with Lee Tillman. Then he'd apologized.

She'd like some insight into his real feelings. But at least she knew that he wanted to keep her safe. Perhaps she should focus on that. Perhaps it meant something more than its face value.

Without looking at him, she murmured, "Okay."

"Okay what?"

"You're right. As long as those guys are out there, I need a bodyguard."

She took in his look of surprise. Probably he'd been expecting an argument, but she wasn't going to give him any.

"Then we'll stop at my house so I can pack some stuff. Then we'll go to yours and do the same."

Once more she agreed.

"My friends Erin and Travis Stone have a vacation retreat down here. I'm pretty sure we can go there."

"What's wrong with Wendy's condo?"

"Nothing. I just don't want to establish a pattern somebody can follow." He continued outlining his plans. "After I get you settled, I'll call a towing service and meet them out at the park. I know your car was running the last time we looked. But I want to make sure it still is."

She expected him to start the engine and pull out of the parking space, but he stayed where he was, looking at her, then said, "I want to ask you a favor."

"What?"

"You've still got the key to Lee Tillman's house?"

"Yes."

"What if we stopped there and looked around for evidence?"

She thought that over. "Would that be illegal? I don't want you to get into trouble again."

"Lee hired me to find out who was harassing him. You have his key. We have a good argument for going in there."

"Then let's get it over with," she murmured, wondering what would happen if they got caught, by Lee or somebody else. And wondering if Alex had made the suggestion because he didn't want to go back into a situation where they'd be alone together with time on their hands.

But she didn't voice that thought.

She expected him to pull into the driveway of The Refuge. Instead, he drove down the road several hundred feet and took an overgrown lane into the woods.

"This is where I parked the day you came in for the files. I figure it's still a good idea," he explained as he pulled up under a low-hanging maple.

She could see the wisdom of that, although it seemed weird when he reached into the glove compartment and pulled out two pairs of latex gloves.

"What are those for?" she asked, hearing her voice rise. "I mean, my fingerprints are already in the house."

"Mine too. But I don't want them everywhere if the police conduct an official investigation."

She nodded tightly, slipping one pair into her purse as they headed toward the rock-strewn shoreline. When she lost her footing as she climbed over a boulder, Alex turned and grabbed her hand.

She held tight to him, keeping her fingers knit with his as they rounded a curve and saw the mansion.

She'd always felt comfortable unlocking the door and

coming in to get papers—until the incident four days ago.
Now it felt strange to fumble in her purse for the key.
Strange to unlock the door and step into the unlit entryway.
Without thinking, she reached for Alex's hand again and
was reassured by the contact with his warm flesh.

"Now what?" she whispered.

"Now we see if we can find anything that will give us
a clue about what happened to Lee."

"Too bad it's such a big house."

"Yeah."

"Maybe we should start with the obvious place—the
office."

As they stepped through the door, her eyes went to the
closet. "You were in there when I came in?" she asked,
gesturing.

"Yeah. And that's where I'm going now. Why don't
you take the file cabinets?"

She did as he asked, feeling as if she was invading Lee's
privacy when she opened a drawer and began to go
through folders.

Lee was a meticulous man, and she found everything
from directions for operating the microwave, to the extended warranty he'd taken out on the heating system, to
five years' worth of bank statements. But there was nothing that gave any indication why he'd disappeared.

When Alex came out of the closet, his expression told
her he hadn't had any better luck.

Turning toward the bookcase in back of the desk, he
started pulling out volumes, holding them spine side up
and shaking them.

Taking her cue from him, she lent a hand. But the search
was only an exercise in futility.

"There are rooms downstairs I've never been in," she

said as she watched Alex shove the last tome back into the bookcase.

His head came up, and he gave her a long look. "Like the art gallery?"

"What art gallery?" she asked, aware that he was watching her carefully.

"It's got some unusual paintings and sculpture."

The tone of his voice made her ask, "You mean of a sexual nature?"

"Yeah."

"Lee showed it to you?"

"I found it when I was here the other day. I was searching for him and stumbled in there. It looked like one of the paintings was missing."

"Did you take it?" she asked.

"Of course not! Why would I tell you about it if I'd taken it?"

She shrugged. "To test me. Every chance you get, you act like you don't believe me."

"It's my old cop habits."

"You're sure it's not more than that?" she asked, hoping he was going to give her a better reason, like he'd caught his wife in a lie and he was having trouble with trust issues.

But he simply shrugged, turned away and started down the hall. She followed him, breezed past and pulled on a door that looked as though it opened into a closet. Instead, there was a flight of stairs leading up.

"The attic?" Alex asked.

"Yes. Lee was putting some stuff up there once when I was here."

Alex felt along the wall and located a light switch. An orange glow warmed the darkness above as they began to climb the stairs. At the top, they both paused to get their bearings.

Like the rest of the house, the attic was neat, with boxes arranged along the perimeter and a fair amount of floor space in the middle.

The air felt hot and dry, but luckily it was too early in the season for serious heat to have built up.

"You take one side, I'll take the other," Alex suggested.

In her present mood, she might have asked if he trusted her to tell him she'd found anything. Instead, she pressed her lips together and bent to the first box. Bold black letters told her it contained Christmas Ornaments. And when she pulled open the flaps, she did indeed find shiny glass balls packed in tissue paper. Rooting through them, she discovered nothing else hidden below the carefully packed layers.

She was looking through a box of canning jars and wondering why Lee had kept them, when an exclamation from Alex made her whirl around.

He had pulled a black and silver, flat-topped metal trunk from the pile of boxes and was sifting through the contents.

"What?" Crossing to him, she saw he was holding up a faded cotton dress. Along the neckline was a dark brown stain.

"That looks like blood," she breathed.

"Yeah."

They both stared at the dress.

"Why would he have that?" she finally asked.

"Good question."

He laid the dress on the lid of the trunk and dug deeper. This time he came up with baby clothes. Two tiny undershirts. Some plastic pants that crinkled when he touched them. Cloth diapers.

To her questioning look, he only shrugged.

Alex's hand was probing the sides of the trunk, when a noise outside made her turn sharply. It sounded like a car had pulled up in front of the house.

"Go see if we've got company," Alex commanded. "Maybe Lee's home."

"And we're poking through his attic," Sara muttered, feeling the blood drain from her face. Quickly she crossed the floor and peered out the dingy window. Her heart started to pound as she spotted a vehicle in the driveway.

"So is it Lee or your friends from the militia?" Alex asked.

"Neither one. It's some guy I don't recognize," she answered, struggling to control her voice.

BEHIND HER, Alex stood up and moved to the window, following the direction of her gaze.

"Lewis Farmer," he muttered.

"Who?"

"He works for Lee. Does handyman jobs," he said, keeping his voice low and even as he pulled her back from the glass, holding her against his side as he angled himself so that his face was barely showing.

"Does he have a key?"

"I guess we'll find out."

She stood there with her pulse pounding, feeling the tension in Alex's body as she thought up good reasons why she was in here wearing a pair of latex gloves. At the moment, none of them made sense.

Aeons dragged by as she waited to find out if the guy was coming inside and marching straight up to the attic. When she finally heard Alex let out a breath, she tipped her head inquiringly toward him.

Before he could answer, she heard an engine start.

"I guess he was just making sure the place was locked up tight," she said.

"Right. But maybe it's time to beat a hasty retreat."

She slid him a sideways look. "Did you, uh, have some kind of run-in with him?"

"Why do you ask?"

"You're kind of tense."

"We go way back. He and I weren't exactly friends in high school."

"He was in another clique?"

Alex gave her a hard look. "Yeah."

She wanted to ask for more details, but his face discouraged any probing.

Striding away, he closed the trunk and looked around the attic before they descended the stairs, closing the door behind them. Then Alex made sure the handyman had really left before leading her to the back door.

Without speaking, they retraced their steps to his SUV, where he backed out of the narrow lane and headed toward his house.

"Why did he pack up a bloody dress and baby clothes?" she asked.

"That's what I'd like to know," he answered, but volunteered no more information.

She looked at the rigid lines of his face, thinking that he'd come to some conclusion that he wasn't prepared to share.

In his driveway, he sat for several moments, staring at the house, and she wanted to break the silence between them. But she didn't know what to say. She'd thought that making love with him might change things between them. But he seemed to have locked it away in a compartment.

Finally he reached for the door handle.

"Wait. You're not really going to eat that stuff you brought back from the restaurant are you?"

He glanced at the carton on the floor. "No, I guess not. We may as well throw it away."

Sara picked up the bag, looking around for trash cans as she joined Alex in the driveway. He was intently inspecting the house and the grounds.

Alex had started up the steps to the porch. Sara was a few paces behind him, when an unexpected noise shattered the afternoon stillness.

It was the sudden sound of loud, angry barking. Not the high-pitched yipping of a pint-size dog. This was the deep, menacing barking of a large animal.

"What the hell?" Alex muttered, whirling to face the sound.

In the next second, a vicious-looking brown and black mongrel came racing toward them from around the side of the house.

Frozen in place, Sara watched it making straight for her, its eyes fierce and its jaw working as if it was anticipating the joy of sinking its teeth into her flesh and tearing her to shreds.

Chapter Eleven

Sara saw Alex whirl toward the animal as he pulled the gun from the waistband of his slacks.

She felt as if she were caught in the eye of a hurricane. Time seemed to shift to slow motion, so that the whole scene hung suspended before her, captured as a single frame on a videotape.

Her fingers tightened around the restaurant bag, and she suddenly remembered what she was holding.

Food. A bag of food.

Her lips moved but no sound came out.

Finally, she found her voice, the word *no* blasting out from her throat in a desperate plea.

With shaking fingers she tore open the bag, pulled up the lid on the container and tossed the contents onto the sidewalk in a rain of french fries, onion rings and hamburger.

As the dog caught the scent of the food, he stopped in his tracks, his head going down to the pavement where he started sniffing avidly, then scarfing up the remains of Alex's lunch.

"Open the door," she gasped.

He was already turning the key in the lock.

Then he barreled down the stairs, caught her under the arms and lifted her off her feet.

Behind her she heard the sounds of frantic eating as Alex carried her across the porch and threw her inside the house.

The dog finished the food and started up the steps behind them, but Alex had already slammed the door.

Cursing loudly, he pushed her toward the floor, then followed her down, his gun still in his hand.

"What? He's not coming through the windows," she gasped out.

"Think about it! That dog didn't come leaping at us until we were out of the truck and walking toward the porch. Those bastards from the militia compound brought him and held him on a leash until they picked their moment to let him loose."

Sara sucked in a shuddering breath as she watched Alex advance toward the back of the house. Keeping low, he moved to the side of a kitchen window and took a cautious look outside.

"I just saw one of them coming toward the house. He probably figures I'd be dog meat by now."

"Your brother?"

"I don't know. You stay back and stay down."

She advanced to the kitchen doorway, watching as he kept his eyes trained on the window. After several seconds, he knocked out a pane of glass with the butt of the gun, then stuck the weapon through the opening and fired.

The shot was returned almost at once. Sara watched in silent disbelief. A couple of days ago she'd asked if he was like a hired gun from the Old West. Now the image came back to haunt her.

He ducked back from the window, turned and saw her in the doorway. "Get back in the hall!"

She couldn't move, couldn't leave him in the kitchen. She'd grown up around here, where hunting for food and sport was part of the normal pattern of life. Probably the men out there had rifles, while Alex only had a handgun.

"Is there a rifle in the house?" she asked.

"Yeah." He didn't take his eyes off the window as he answered. "Up in my bedroom. In the right side of the closet. The ammunition's in the top dresser drawer."

She took a deep breath and started back down the hall, moving quickly, keeping low. Still bent over, she dashed up the stairs and into the room where he slept. The closet was to the left of the door. The rifle was where he'd said it would be.

From outside she heard another round fired. Then more glass breaking inside the house and the sound of Alex's gun.

Sprinting to the dresser, she opened the drawer. But someone outside must have seen her through the window, because a bullet crashed through the wall and into the room.

She heard herself scream but she stayed in the room long enough to open the drawer and find the shells. Then she dashed back the way she'd come.

Outside, the dog was barking as he raced back and forth along the porch, jumping at the windows and the door. When he saw her, he threw his body against one of the living-room windows, but the glass held.

Alex was crouched beside a set of shattered glass panes.

Looking back at her, he ordered, "Stay down and slide me the rifle and the box of bullets. Then get back into the hall and call Hempstead," he said, reeling off the number. "Tell him I made a mistake about not pressing charges."

She did as he asked, watching him load the weapon, then move to another window.

Creeping into the hall, she picked up the pocketbook she'd dropped on the floor, found her cell phone and dialed.

More shots sounded as she reached the chief.

"What the hell is going on?" Hempstead asked.

"We're at Alex's house. And the militia's here! They sent a dog to tear us apart as we climbed out of the car. When that didn't work, they started shooting."

"On our way," Hempstead informed her and hung up.

The shooting stopped, the sound of silence strangely unreal.

Crunching across broken glass, Sara kept below the window level as she moved to Alex's side. "Are you hurt?" she asked, relieved when she saw no blood on his clothing.

"I'm fine. I think I got one of them. Well, he was still on his feet, but I could see he was wounded. I think the yellow-bellied bastards are cutting their losses." He glanced away from the window for a moment and scowled at her. "But I told you to stay the hell out of here."

She nodded tightly, needing to be with him. Needing to feel the warmth of his body pressed to hers. But she knew that he had to keep his full attention on the scene outside, in case the shooters' withdrawal was just a ploy to get him to lower his guard. So she moved back to the hall doorway, her ears trained toward the woods that bordered the stream.

There were no more shots. It seemed that once the bad guys realized that Alex was going to keep shooting, they'd turned and run.

The dog was another matter. He was still outside on the front porch, barking and throwing himself against the windows, trying to get in. If he found the shattered window in back, they were in trouble.

Alex's thoughts must be taking the same turn as hers. "There's lunch meat in the refrigerator. And some fried chicken. Get it," he shouted as he turned and pounded up the steps.

Moments later he was back with a bottle of capsules.

He rolled one inside several pieces of meat, then slipped another under the chicken skin.

Back in the living room, he put the chain on the door, moving back as the dog lunged for the opening, his jaw snapping.

"Easy, boy. Easy," he said. "Don't those jerks feed you? Want some more dinner?"

Avoiding the dog's snapping teeth, he tossed the chicken onto the porch. When the dog had wolfed it down, he followed it with the luncheon meat.

"What did you give him?"

"Sleeping pills."

"You need sleeping pills?"

"The doctor prescribed them. I didn't like the effect so I only took a couple."

"Alex..."

"Let's not focus on medications," he said in a thick voice. Moving toward her, he pulled her into his arms. There was no thought of resistance. She melted against him, closing her eyes as she listened to the sound of sirens in the distance.

Minutes later, two patrol cars rolled into the driveway and pulled in front of the house. Hempstead and two deputies climbed out. One's name tag said Sullivan. The other, Garnette.

One of the men jumped back when he spotted the brute of a dog. But the animal was lying on his side, eyes closed, breathing evenly.

The deputies eyed her and Alex suspiciously. She met their stares head-on. Probably they were remembering that Alex had just been released from jail yesterday morning and now he was in trouble again. No doubt they were assuming it was his own damn fault—until they found out otherwise.

"What the hell happened?" the chief demanded as he moved cautiously toward the porch.

"Like Sara told you. The militia brought over an attack dog to tear us up. You might want to get him to a vet. He's had a couple of adult-size sleeping pills."

"They won't kill him," the chief answered. "Unless he's been guzzling them along with booze."

"His handlers were waiting back in the woods," Alex said.

"You saw them?"

He nodded. "Three or four of them." He led the way through the house and into the kitchen.

The chief whistled when he saw the broken glass and bullet holes. "Looks like you had yourself a little fire-fight," he commented.

"Yeah. Out on the public road when they attacked Sara, they stuck with handguns. Back here where they couldn't be seen, they brought out something a little more serious. I imagine the owners of the house aren't going to be too pleased. I guess I'd better arrange to get the windows boarded up."

"I'll get a crime-scene team out here," the chief said. "And see what we can find out about the weapons."

"There's a bullet somewhere upstairs, too," Sara told him.

Alex whirled toward her, a curse on his lips. "You forgot to mention that to me!"

"I'm fine," she told him. Then, ignoring his scowl, she gestured toward the stairs as she explained to the chief, "Alex sent me up to get his rifle. I guess they saw me through the window."

"I think it's time to reevaluate pressing charges," Alex growled.

The chief nodded. "I think it's time to pay a visit to the old Fairmont Estate."

"I'd like to go along," Alex said.

"This is official police business."

"Yeah, well, they just paid *me* a visit."

"You can't be sure it was them."

"I think I can make an educated guess."

The chief nodded.

Alex looked from Hempstead to Sara and back again. "The trouble is, I can't take her along. And I haven't had time to talk to Erin Stone about borrowing her place."

Sara angled her chin upward. "I thought I made it clear that I don't like the two of you discussing my safety as if I'm not here. I can go back to Wendy's condo. I'm sure she wouldn't mind my staying at her place while you guys go off and do the dangerous stuff."

Alex considered her suggestion. He didn't like it for the reason he'd previously given. And he didn't like leaving her alone when she'd already been in danger twice today. On the other hand, at the moment, he liked the Stone place even less. Because it was isolated, and if the bad guys found her there alone, she'd be a sitting duck.

"You're planning to go over to the militia compound as soon as possible?" Alex asked Hempstead.

"I've already done an evaluation of the place, so I think it's safe to go in."

An evaluation of the place. That was news to Alex. But then, he was finding out a lot of interesting things this week about Chief Hempstead and about life in the peaceful little community of St. Stephens.

"I've studied photographs of the layout," Hempstead continued. "I've done an electronics sweep, so I know they don't have an early-warning system. They rely on a guarded gatehouse at the entrance road. I've done a topographical assessment, and I know there's only one road in and out of the place. And not much natural cover, unless you want to get down into the marshland along the river.''

"Glad you did your homework," Alex answered. "When did you finish?"

"Less than two weeks ago, so I assume the situation hasn't changed. As soon as I can get a couple of extra deputies, we'll pay them a visit. I've let this thing go on unchecked too long. They haven't made any real trouble until now, but I'm not going to stand for this kind of violence," he said, sweeping his hand toward the bullet holes in the walls.

"If I take Sara down to her friend's condo, will you wait for me?" He knew the request was outrageous. The police didn't have to wait for a private citizen before making a visit to town troublemakers. But he figured the chief owed him one.

Apparently Hempstead had the same opinion, because he nodded.

Alex went upstairs and grabbed the overnight bag he kept packed for emergencies. Then, as they all stepped onto the porch, another problem presented itself. They had forgotten about the dog, and he was still lying there on his side, snoring loudly. Alex looked at the massive jaw now relaxed in sleep. When the brute woke up, he was going to be a menace, particularly since his handlers had disappeared. He needed to be in a secure cage.

Hempstead turned to Sullivan. "You call animal control, then meet me—"

"At The Refuge," Alex suggested, neglecting to mention that he'd been there earlier. "It's the next estate over from the militia enclave."

"That's a plan." Hempstead looked at his watch. "We can meet at 1800 hours. That way we'll still have plenty of daylight left."

"Do you want extra help?" Alex asked. "Randolph Security will send down four or five men by helicopter if I ask for backup."

The chief thought about it. "I appreciate the offer, but I'm not really thinking of this as a tactical situation. They may have come gunning for you because this is an isolated location. But I don't think even the People's Militia are dumb enough to attack the police and think they can get away with it."

Alex hoped Hempstead was right, but he wasn't going to argue. While the deputy made the call about the dog, he escorted Sara to his SUV.

He was still thinking about her getting shot at when she'd gone up to retrieve the rifle. And he had to clamp his hands around the steering wheel to keep from reaching for her in front of the chief and the deputy.

"I'm sorry," he said.

"For what?"

"For taking you to my house." He gave a sharp, ironic laugh. "I guess Billy warned me."

"Neither one of us was expecting something like this."

"I should have been." He sighed. "I keep making bad judgment calls."

"I think your judgment is fine. I'd say you've just hit a streak of rotten luck. We both have, actually. Maybe Mercury is retrograde or something."

"What does that mean?"

"I was hoping you might know. I have a friend who's into astrology who blames everything from a broken fingernail to the stock market plunge on it."

He laughed. After that, they rode in silence for several minutes until she asked, "What are you thinking about?"

"Tactics. Logistics." He studied the rearview mirror again. As far as he could tell, they weren't being followed.

More silent miles passed, and his thoughts turned to the baby clothes in the attic trunk. He'd started off thinking that Lee and Sara might have been having an affair. Now he wondered if the man was her natural father. A big stretch, he silently admitted. But the idea did have some resonance. It would certainly explain why Lee had been a hell of a lot nicer to Sara Delaney than he was to most people. Of course, that didn't explain the dress with the blood. But he might get some answers when he had a chance to examine the letters he'd pulled out of the trunk while Sara had gone to the window.

The letters were in his overnight bag now, and he felt slightly guilty about concealing them, but he wanted to have his ducks in a row before saying anything to her.

After reaching the downtown district, he drove back to the condo. Quickly he ushered Sara inside, then crossed to the drapes and drew them closed.

He turned to find her watching him with an expression of concern.

"I'll be back before you know it," he said.

She took a step toward him. "Alex, you don't have to go with Chief Hempstead. The police can take care of it."

"What am I supposed to do, hole up until the excitement's over?"

"Like me, you mean."

He snorted. "Those bastards were going to do God knows what to you! Then they tried to kill us. I'm going to be in on whatever happens."

"Are you trying to prove something?"

"I don't have to prove anything. I just have to maintain

my self-respect.'' Before she could make some other dumb comment, he turned and stalked toward the door.

"Lock up. And don't let anybody but me or the police in.''

"What are you going to do when you get to the militia compound, start shooting?''

"Not unless they do.'' Of course, they'd done it before, so it wasn't out of the question, but he didn't point that out. In fact, he left before she could come up with some other argument. Obviously she didn't get it. Every step of the way in this case, somebody was either using him or screwing with him, and he wanted a chance to turn the tables.

But that didn't mean he was going to play cowboy, because if he made the wrong move, he could get himself—or somebody else—killed.

THREE POLICE CARS were parked around the bend of Lee Tillman's driveway. Alex pulled up in back of the cruisers and stepped out, aware that all eyes were on him.

For two days he'd worn an orange prison jumpsuit. Now he was going with the cops to pay an official visit to the men who had been shooting at him and Sara.

Probably all the officers confronting him were thinking about that.

Chief Hempstead stepped forward. "This is Alex Shane,'' he said. "He used to be a Howard County detective. He got himself in a little trouble with the law a few days ago, but that's all straightened out. He's the kind of guy you like to have around in a tight spot. This morning he drove off two armed militiamen who were set to attack an unarmed woman. This afternoon he did it again—only it was three or four armed men and an attack dog.''

The men had probably heard the account before, but

they looked suitably impressed with his prowess. He didn't spoil the impression by pointing out that Sara had distracted the dog with his lunch long enough for them to get into the house.

"Alex, you've already met Dick Sullivan and Tim Garnette. These are Paul Wallace and Hank Carpenter."

"Good to meet you," Alex said, appreciating the chief's show of confidence in him. Dick and Paul were the seasoned veterans. Tim and Hank looked as if they'd just graduated from high school. He wondered how much tactical experience they'd had, how reliable they'd be if trouble broke out.

"So let's get the ground rules straight," Hempstead said. "We're going to be super cautious. We don't start anything. We're nice and polite. We're just looking into the possibility that the individuals who were shooting at Alex might be associated with the People's Militia. And while we're on their property, we're keeping our eyes and ears open. We're estimating how many of them are actually out there, what kind of facilities they have, if there are weapons in evidence. Got it?"

There were murmurs and nods of agreement around the circle.

"You're with me," Paul Wallace said to Alex.

He climbed into the front seat of the police car, remembering his recent ride in the back of a similar vehicle. The other men boarded the remaining cars. Hempstead drove the lead cruiser, with Alex and Wallace next.

Neither Alex nor the driver bothered with small talk. In fact, now that they were heading for the militia camp, Alex felt his throat tighten. These guys had given Sara nothing but trouble. On the first day he'd seen her, one of them had tried to run her over. And it had only gotten worse.

All his senses were alert as they turned off the highway

and onto the access road decorated with Keep Out signs. The lane was narrow. On either side, the late-afternoon sun shone on fields overgrown with weeds. He could see the remnants of landscaping, but the bushes were choked with Virginia creeper and dead branches lay where they had fallen off trees.

A shadow flickered at the edge of his vision, and he automatically reached toward his gun. Then he saw it was only a trio of crows pecking at something hidden in the tall grass.

About a hundred yards up the road, the convoy came to a small building with a metal roof, shingled siding and a large sliding window facing the road.

A sign said: Halt. That means you. Have identification ready. Trespassers will be shot.

Friendly, Alex thought.

Hempstead pulled to a stop and got out, but there was no uniformed militiaman waiting to check his identification. The small building was empty.

The chief looked back at Alex where he sat in the second car. He shrugged, fighting a prickle of uneasiness at the base of his neck.

Climbing back into his car, Hempstead led the way slowly up the road.

The farther they proceeded, the more Alex's sense of disquiet increased. He didn't know what he expected to find, but he was sure now that it wasn't going to be good.

Several low, beige buildings came into view as they rounded a curve. They were new and rough-looking. Thrown up by the militia, he guessed.

A Humvee was pulled up near the large double doorway of one building.

Hempstead halted again. This time everyone climbed out.

Alex knew he wasn't the only one feeling tense as he looked at the faces of the officers around him.

Hempstead stepped inside the structure and was gone for several seconds. "It's a garage," he announced. "There are a few trucks inside. That's all."

They started up again, this time heading for the old mansion house. Alex's first impression was that the white siding needed repair and painting. Some of the shingles were missing, as were several of the faded green shutters. But there were no men in view and an eerie quiet hung heavy in the air.

Alex got the first inkling of real trouble when Paul Wallace braked abruptly, then pointed toward a clump of bushes about fifty feet from the house.

Chapter Twelve

Alex followed the man's outstretched arm and saw a pair of black boots sticking out from the foliage. As they inched closer he saw legs clad in black pants.

Opening the door, he drew his weapon and stepped out. Paul had radioed the rest of the cars, and the column of three vehicles halted.

Officers exited the cruisers, covering Alex as he made his way toward the bushes. Drawing closer, he saw a short, compact man sprawled facedown in the dirt. Dressed in a black uniform, he held a pistol in his right hand. A trio of stains marred the back of his uniform shirt, and blood pooled in the dirt around his torso. The congealed liquid and the flies told Alex that the guy had been there for several hours.

Hempstead and Dick Sullivan entered the mansion. Alex and the rest of the officers fanned out around the property, moving cautiously. He saw two more bodies. One was dressed in the black uniform, another in a redneck outfit like the ones Billy and his partner had sported that morning.

He had rounded the corner of the house when the chief exited the back door and spotted him. The look on the veteran police officer's face warned him to prepare for something bad.

"What?" he asked sharply.

"I'm sorry. Your brother's in there."

"Dead?"

"Yes."

Alex felt his throat close. All he could do was give a tight nod. Since spotting the first dead militiaman in the bushes, he'd been prepared for something awful. Now the chief had confirmed the worst.

"How many others are inside?" he managed to ask.

"Fifteen. All dead."

"Where's Billy?"

"You don't have to look at him now. You can identify the body later."

"I need to see what happened. Where is he?"

"In the family room, I guess you'd call it."

Alex pushed past the chief and strode into the house. He saw black-clad figures in various locations, but he didn't stop to examine them as he stalked down the hall, following the sounds of a ball game coming from the interior of the house.

He found his brother and another guy sprawled on a sofa, their feet up on a low coffee table. Billy had been holding a glass of beer. The amber brew had spilled onto the sofa and his shirt, mixing with the blood. His brother hadn't even gotten a chance to draw his weapon.

Hempstead was right behind him. "I'm sorry," he said again.

"I kept thinking he was going to come to a bad end. I didn't quite imagine this," Alex answered as he stood staring at his brother—at the look of surprise on his face.

For long seconds he was rooted to the spot. Then he

turned and expelled a heaving breath. "What do you think happened?"

The chief looked as shocked as Alex felt. But his answer came out clear and thoughtful. "Could be an invading force mowed them down. A rival militia. Or one faction might have gone after the other. These groups aren't always the most stable environment. A lot of crazies and violent types join. Put that together with their firepower, and you've got trouble."

"Yeah." Suddenly Alex felt very tired.

"It could be that one guy or a couple of them went berserk," the chief added. "We need to find out if all the victims belong to the militia, how many are accounted for and how many are missing. I'm calling in a team from the state police crime lab. Until they're done, I want the whole area cordoned off. I'll send one of my cars down to guard the gate. Another team will secure the river area. We're going to be here for a while, but there's no need for you to stay. In fact, maybe you want to be out of the way before the state police arrive." The chief made a throat-clearing noise. "Not that you're a suspect or anything. I know where you've been pretty much all day."

Alex realized he was still holding his Glock and slipped the weapon back into its holster.

"We haven't found Tripp Kenney, the guy who commanded this place. Which doesn't mean he's not here," the chief said.

Alex nodded. "I'd appreciate a ride back to The Refuge."

"Give me a couple of minutes. I'd like a body count before it gets too dark to see what we're doing. How many did you find?" he asked.

"Three. The first guy Wallace spotted and two more. I can mark the spots for you."

"Thanks."

The chief called his men back to the area in front of the house. In all, they'd discovered twenty-six bodies, mostly on the first floor of the mansion. Kenney was not among the dead.

After Alex had marked the location of the two additional victims he'd discovered, Wallace drove him back to his car.

It was a silent ride in the gathering darkness—a mixed blessing as far as Alex was concerned. He didn't want to keep up a conversation, yet that might have distracted him from a thousand memories that assaulted him.

He and Billy as little kids riding their bikes to the 7-Eleven for Slushies. Swimming in the river. Catching crayfish in the creek. Snitching candy from the drugstore. Stealing hubcaps. Breaking windows at the school.

The few times he'd visited his brother in the state penitentiary years ago had been bad. They were nothing compared to that last awful image—his brother sprawled in a pool of blood and beer on a fake-leather sofa.

He squeezed his eyes shut, trying to banish that sight. Maybe the chief was right. Maybe he shouldn't have looked. He'd seen plenty of victims of violent murders, and he'd thought he was prepared. He'd been wrong.

When he felt the car come to a halt, his eyes snapped open, and he was surprised to find that twilight had descended over the landscape. Wallace had pulled up beside his SUV.

"Thanks for the ride," he told the officer.

"No problem."

The man cleared his throat. "I'm sorry it worked out this way."

"Yes," Alex answered. "Thanks." Did you say thanks

under circumstances like this? he wondered. He didn't know.

The officer waited while Alex started up the truck, then they both glided down the driveway, their headlights cutting through the thickening darkness.

Wallace turned in the direction of the estate, a long night ahead of him. Alex turned toward town. The idea flashed into his mind that he'd like to just keep driving right through St. Stephens—all the way back to Baltimore.

But then what? Leaving this place wouldn't erase the image of his brother's body from his mind.

He wanted to be alone. But he couldn't simply leave Sara in her friend's condo with no transportation.

So he pulled himself together long enough to check the rearview mirror to make sure he wasn't being followed, then headed for the waterfront.

As he cut the engine and switched off his headlights, a thought struck him. Since the militia had been coming after Sara and now a lot of them were dead, did that eliminate the threat to her? He didn't know, but he hoped so.

He'd thought he wanted to be alone, but he found himself hurrying toward the concrete stairs. When he knocked on the door, Sara answered almost immediately.

"Who is it?"

"Alex."

She threw the door open, her gaze taking him in as he stood under the dim utility light.

"Oh God, Alex, what happened?"

He stepped inside the condo and closed the door behind him. Then he felt the strength go out of his knees. As he collapsed back against the door, Sara propelled herself forward and reached for him.

She locked her arms around his middle, pressed her cheek against his shoulder and held on to him.

Nothing had ever felt so comforting as the reassurance of her tight clasp or the warmth of her breath filtering through his shirt and spreading across his skin. Once more he closed his eyes, his own arms coming up to gather her closer.

"Can you tell me what happened?" she murmured.

He tried. In short, disjointed phrases that hardly made sense to his own ears, he told her about the carnage—and about his brother.

She responded with soft exclamations. "Oh God, Alex. It must have been terrible." As she spoke, her hands smoothed across his back, over his shoulders.

He felt a sob welling from deep in his chest, one heaving sob before he regained some measure of control. Still, he felt himself shaking with the effort.

SARA LIFTED her head, her eyes seeking Alex's. She had been frightened for him the whole time he'd been away. She was still frightened. Sensing that he wanted to look away, she strove to hold him with her gaze.

"It's okay," she repeated. "It's okay to grieve for him, to feel helpless and sad and angry. It's okay to let yourself feel it."

He swallowed convulsively as he brought his hands up and set her away from him. "I let him down. He got all screwed up, and I should have straightened him out."

"You were just a kid. Kids can't do that for each other."

"What do you know about it?" he demanded, his voice rising in volume, his hands clenching into fists. "You never had a little brother."

If he was trying to drive her away, it wasn't going to work. "Alex, I know you've just been through a terrible experience. But stop beating yourself up," she said softly.

"You weren't responsible for your brother's problems. You had enough of a job being responsible for yourself. You'd dug yourself into your own hole, and you pulled yourself out."

"No," he answered, fighting her. Fighting logic.

The pain in his eyes was stronger than the defiance. Her own need to wipe away that pain was almost overwhelming. But she knew there was no way to breach the gap between them with words. She had already tried them and failed. In fact, the only time she'd really sensed that she was communicating with him was when they'd made love.

Desperate for him to understand that she would stand by him until the end of time and beyond, she closed the small space that he had put between them, lifted her head and brought her mouth to his.

His instant reaction was resistance, and she felt her spirit contract. Then, from one heartbeat to the next, his lips changed from hard to soft and she knew she had won.

On a groan, he gathered her to him, his mouth almost savage as it moved over hers.

Yes, Alex. Yes. Take anything you want from me, she silently urged, her hands clasping him to her as she opened for him, telling him every way she could that she was his.

She felt his need spiraling up. Need that matched her own. Dizzy with it, she angled her mouth, devouring him even as he did the same. Her hands began to move restlessly over his back, under his shirt, stroking the hot skin she found there, warming her palms on him, the heat sinking into every cell of her body.

He broke away from her and dragged his shirt over his head, tossing it onto the carpet before removing his gun and setting it on a nearby table. Then his hands went to the front of her shirt, pulling at buttons.

She helped him, starting from the bottom, their hands meeting under her breasts.

He pushed the shirt off her shoulders, then reached for the catch of her bra, and she knew that if she didn't stop them, they'd be rolling together on the rug.

"Wait."

He made a sound of protest, but she only took his hand and led him down the hall to the darkened bedroom.

There was enough light from the hallway to see the harsh lines of his face as she reached for him again.

The world seemed to contract around her. There was only this man, this place, this need.

She felt his hands trembling as they took up where they'd left off. Lifting her bra out of the way, he caught her breasts in his hands, cradling them, kneading them, pleasuring them.

Her own hands trembled as she pushed down her slacks and panties, then kicked them aside. He had done the same, so that they were both naked when he pulled her body against his and brought his mouth back to hers for a deep, hungry kiss.

She kissed him with equal intensity, wanting with all her being to give him what he needed tonight, to lose her identity in kisses and touches and soft sounds of desire.

When he pulled her down to the surface of the bed, she felt a fierce surge of joy as they rocked together, kissed each other, touched all the places that begged to be touched, building the fire to a white-hot, unbearable intensity.

He surged into her then, his hips setting a sharp frantic rhythm that carried her up one jagged incline after another, then sent her toppling over the edge, the shock of her release so intense that she gasped out her pleasure.

She felt his body shudder above hers, heard his cry mingle with hers. Then she was clinging to him, rocking him in her arms, trying to tell him without words what their joining had meant to her.

She thought he might leave her then and withdraw into himself the way he had the last time. But after what he had been through all that long, long day, he must not have had the strength. Moments later, she felt the even rhythm of his breathing and knew he was sleeping. She eased away from him enough to reach for the quilt at the bottom of the bed and pulled it over them. Then she settled down beside him in the darkness, feeling her own grip on consciousness loosened.

THE SMELL OF COFFEE brewing and bacon cooking woke Alex. His eyes opened and he peered around at the unfamiliar bedroom.

Then memory came swooping back. Sara. Warm, generous Sara. He had taken everything she'd offered last night, and he wasn't sure what he was capable of giving in return.

He remembered the pain of seeing Billy dead. Remembered his guilt. Remembered Sara taking him in her arms and wiping all the bad stuff away. More than that she replaced it with lovemaking so good that he had to stop and catch his breath even now.

And this morning she was out in the kitchen making him breakfast. Either that or she'd hired a caterer.

He pushed himself up and saw his overnight bag sitting on the floor. Apparently, she'd brought it in from the SUV. His hands clenched. Had she looked in it and found the letters he'd hidden there?

He pulled his mind away from that direction. She wasn't Cindy! She wouldn't snoop.

But she would take chances—like going out to buy groceries. His face contorted. One of the militiamen might still be out there stalking her. But they hadn't talked about that last night. Actually, they hadn't talked about much.

He wanted to stride down the hall and upbraid her for leaving the condo. But he wasn't sure he could face her yet, and he wasn't sure a tongue-lashing was even justified.

So he climbed out of bed and took the overnight bag into the bathroom. The papers he'd taken from the trunk in Lee Tillman's attic were still on the bottom where he'd put them.

After showering, shaving and dressing, he couldn't postpone the inevitable any longer. When he entered the kitchen, he found Sara looking expectantly toward the door. She smoothed her hands down the sides of her hips as he approached, and he couldn't stop himself from following the gesture with his eyes.

She wasn't dressed in the slacks and shirt from last night, he noted. Instead, she was wearing a soft cotton shift with a paisley pattern that flowed around her body when she walked.

"Where did you get the dress?" he asked.

"At one of the shops in town."

"Going out wasn't such a good idea."

She cleared her throat. "With the militia...uh... disabled...I figured I could take the chance."

"Some of them are still on the loose. At least one that we know of." Tripp Kenney, the leader, was still at large.

She gave a tight nod, then pointed toward the coffeepot. "You want some?"

"Yeah. You bought groceries, too?"

"Uh-huh." She poured him a mug and set it on the table.

"So half the town saw you this morning. Anybody could have figured out where you were staying."

"Don't worry, I didn't tell them I was shacked up with you."

"That's not what I meant."

She turned back to the stove and began transferring scrambled eggs to a serving plate that already held the bacon.

The table was set, so he pulled out the nearest chair and sat down, watching her bring the food. The easy domesticity made him nervous—as if she was making some sort of claim on him.

"How do you feel?" she asked.

"Like hell."

"You didn't sleep well?"

"I slept fine, thanks to you. The point is, you're not supposed to leave the scene where your brother was shot and go home and have great sex."

As soon as he saw the softening of her features, he regretted the hasty observation.

"Was it?" she murmured.

"You know damn well it was. And we both know—"

She cut him off before he could finish. "And one of us understands that it's okay to turn to somebody who cares about you when you're in pain."

"So she can administer emotional first aid?"

"Stop it!" she said, her voice rising. "I'm getting tired of your acting like we don't mean anything to each other."

He rocked back in his chair, then let the front legs hit the floor with a thump.

He felt trapped. And guilty. And at the same time, he felt like a rat.

He was looking down into his coffee cup when she pulled out her chair and joined him at the table. He watched her dish up eggs and transfer a slice of bacon to her plate.

She took a small bite of eggs, chewed and swallowed before saying, "Alex, I care about you. And I want to be here for you. If you can't accept that from me, I'll deal with it."

"Sara, it's not you. It's me."

"I think I've heard that brush-off before," she said in a low voice.

"It's not a brush-off. I'm going through some stuff that's made me…cautious." He dragged in a breath and let it out slowly, thinking that stonewalling wasn't doing him much good. "I caught my wife with another man. That kind of makes you careful about leaping into new relationships."

"I can understand that," she said in a low voice.

He studied her face. She didn't exactly look surprised, more like relieved.

"Did you already know that?" he demanded.

She sighed. "I'm not much good at lying. Your friend Dan Cassidy told me."

"Did he? So this is a case of mercy screwing. The poor guy walked in on his wife with another guy so you want him to think he's not a total loser."

"I was pretty sure you'd jump to that conclusion," she snapped. "But you're dead wrong. I wasn't screwing you. I was making love with you—in case you can't tell the difference. Which apparently you can't. So I might as well quit while I'm ahead."

She pushed back her chair and started for the door.

"Where the hell do you think you're going?" he demanded, climbing to his feet.

"Home."

His reaction was swift and primal. "No, you're not. Not with a possible contingent of militiamen still on the loose. You're staying where I can protect you. And that means somewhere safe—now that you've blown our cover with this apartment.''

She stood with her hands on her hips, glaring at him. "You're not ordering me around! Not with your attitude.''

He forced himself to calm down, forced himself to speak in a normal voice when he still wanted to shout at her. "You said you care about me. Well, I care about you, too.'' It was difficult to say the words, but he got them out.

"You have a strange way of showing it.''

He turned his palm upward. "Okay. I'm not in such great shape. Remember, I just saw my brother's dead body laid out in a pool of beer and blood.''

She winced, her face instantly filling with concern, and he hated himself for using underhanded tactics. Yes, he'd been pretty shook up yesterday, but this present conversation had nothing to do with his brother. He was using Billy because he understood on some deep, instinctive level that he'd use anything to keep her from walking out the door.

"Alex,'' she murmured, taking a step toward him.

He couldn't admit that he wanted anything from her besides keeping her safe. But as she came toward him, he opened his arms and reached for her, folding her close.

For long moments he simply held on to her as she leaned into him. Then he muttered, "I'm asking you to let me stay with you.''

His pulse pounded in his ears as he waited for her to say yes or no.

"If that's what you want to do,'' she finally answered, and he let out the breath he was holding.

"Yes.''

"Then you have to let me help you.''

"With what?'' he answered, instantly on guard.

"With anything you need. Like planning Billy's funeral. Can I help you with that?"

"Yes. Thank you." He'd only been nineteen when his mom had died, and he'd let Aunt Greta take care of the details. He hadn't known how to handle the arrangements back then. He still didn't. Relieved and grateful to have someone share the responsibility, he let Sara start making phone calls. After talking to one of the local funeral directors, she was able to offer him options and give suggestions, although she always let him make the final decisions.

But he was too restless to sit still. Too restless to stay in the same room with her for long. So two days later he told her he needed to make a research trip to Baltimore. Then he left her with her father for eight hours, feeling guilty but at the same time relieved to have some breathing space. When he finally got to the city he started working on the envelopes he'd found in the trunk. They were to a woman named Callie Anderson from her father, saying he was sorry and begging her to come home because her mother was dying.

First he tried the address on Blackwood Street, where Callie had been living when she'd received the letter. But the whole block of buildings had been torn down. So he went back to the return address, where he assumed she'd lived before she moved away from home, since the letter was from her father. The residence was a redbrick row house in Canton, near the Baltimore waterfront. From what he could gather, the Anderson family had moved away long ago. He started knocking on doors, anyway, up and down the street, around the corner and across the alley. When he was about ready to give up, he found a crotchety old man, a Mr. Simmons, who remembered the family.

What he had to say was unsettling. According to Sim-

mons, the father had been abusive to his daughters, Callie
and Lacy, beating them and taking them to task verbally
at the slightest excuse.''

"Physical and verbal abuse?" Alex asked.

"Yes and maybe worse."

"Sexual abuse?" Alex pressed.

The old man nodded. "Back in those days, nobody
talked about stuff like that. But the way those girls acted,
I thought something was going on with their father.''

"How did they behave?"

"Shy one minute, seductive the next—like they didn't
know how to deal with men.''

Alex nodded, picturing it as the old man added more
details.

"They both ran away from home. Callie took up with
some rich guy who got her pregnant and then abandoned
her. She died. Maybe Lacy did too. Or she moved far
away. I haven't seen her in years, I know that. But some
other guy came around here asking about Lacy once—
about ten years ago.''

Alex's ears pricked up. "Another guy?"

"Yeah. A little fellow. He was kind of gruff. Kind of
strange, you know. Like he knew more about the girls than
he was saying.''

Who the hell was that? Alex wondered.

He tried another question. "What happened to the
baby?"

"I guess she was put up for adoption. I don't know
anything about that.''

"You know it was a girl?"

"That's what I heard. Don't know for sure, 'cause we
never saw her around here.''

Alex asked a few more questions, but Mr. Simmons had
given him everything he could.

"Well, I appreciate the help."

The old man nodded. "It was a long time ago. But I remember right well."

Alex's next stop was back at 43 Light Street, where he visited the offices of Birth Data, Inc. Erin Stone gave him an exasperated look when he said he was still trying to track down the girl baby from St. Stephens. "Alex, I can't tell you who it was," she said.

"Just a couple of questions. Weren't most of the babies put up for adoption by their mothers?"

"Yes."

"So was this case different? Did a man put the child up for adoption?"

She got up, went to a file cabinet and consulted some papers.

"It was a woman."

"Thanks," he said, sighing.

"That wasn't any help?"

"I was hoping I was on the trail of the father. I guess not."

THE FUNERAL WAS three days later, on one of those raw spring days when you wished you were inside watching flames dance over burning logs in the fireplace, Alex thought as he stood under a cold, leaden sky staring at his brother's plain wooden casket.

He'd known that Billy would want as little fuss as possible, so he'd arranged a simple graveside service.

Of course, since he hadn't been to church in years, Alex hadn't even known whom to ask to officiate. Sara, a member of the Methodist church, had arranged for her minister to say some words over Billy's grave in the family plot next to their mother.

Not many people attended. Some of their friends from

the old days came, and some other people from town. He wasn't sure whether they were there for him or Billy or for Sara.

One thing he was glad he didn't have to worry about was security. Chief Hempstead had a contingent of men surrounding them, making sure that no stragglers from the People's Militia crashed the service. He knew now, from the chief's investigations, that at least fifteen of them were out there somewhere. But none of them had been seen around town.

There were no hymns at the service. If they'd been in church, there would have been hymns, Alex thought with a little pang of regret. Billy had liked "Amazing Grace." He could have sung that for his brother. It was one of the few pieces of church music he remembered.

The minister was speaking, asking for a moment of silent prayer.

Alex bowed his head, and he asked the Lord's forgiveness—for his brother's transgressions and for his own.

As he watched the casket being lowered into the grave, he felt his vision blur. Lord, Billy had been so young. So unsure of himself. So shortchanged by life. And he had deserved a second chance—which he was never going to get. When he felt Sara's fingers close around his, he grasped her tightly, holding on because he needed to hold tightly to someone.

No, not someone. Sara. The realization sent a wave of terror through him.

She felt him shiver and strengthened her grip.

He squeezed his eyes shut. After Cindy, he had sworn that he was never going to let himself depend on anyone besides himself. Now he knew he wasn't strong enough to keep that vow. He needed Sara. At least at this moment he could admit that he needed her, because he felt as if he might drift away from the earth if he wasn't anchored to her.

Chapter Thirteen

Finally, mercifully, the service was over. When the minister approached, Alex mumbled some words of thanks. As he turned away from the grave, he saw Margaret Weston looking at him. She'd been a friend of his mother's, and when she came up and hugged him, he held her for a moment.

"I'm so sorry," she murmured.

"Thanks." He still wasn't sure if that was the right thing to say, but he'd been repeating it often enough over the past few days.

"I knew you couldn't have murdered Emmett Bandy," she said. "I'm glad they released you so fast."

"Yes. Thanks," he said again.

She squeezed his arm, then stepped aside so that others could greet him.

Several old acquaintances made a point of coming up to him. He tried not to act as if he wanted to get away as he let them express their sympathy. Then he was finally alone again.

Feeling as though he'd run a gauntlet, he sighed as he looked around for Sara.

"Are you okay?" she asked as she moved to his side.

"Yeah."

He'd taken several steps toward the road, when he saw a short, slender woman about fifteen feet away moving to intercept his path. He blinked. It was Dana Eustice, Lee Tillman's girlfriend. He certainly hadn't expected her to be here.

Today she wore a taupe-colored leather coat with a fake leopard-skin collar. Her blond hair must have been anchored in place with hair spray, he thought, since not a strand moved in the wind. Her face was carefully made up, as though she were attending a party rather than a funeral.

She flicked her eyes to Sara, and he saw a disdainful look cross her features. Before he could analyze it, she closed the distance between them and started speaking.

"Alex, I was so sorry to hear about your brother," she said in a low voice.

"Thank you," he answered with his stock phrase.

"I'm sorry Lee couldn't be here," she added.

He searched her face. "*I'm* sorry Lee seems to have disappeared."

Her response was instantaneous. "Well, that's because of the Bandy murder."

"Oh?"

"He was at Bandy's office that morning. Now he's afraid the police will try to pin it on him—like they tried to pin it on you."

"I thought you said he was on his way to Nova Scotia. He never arrived at his hotel. And I asked my office to check along his route. There are no credit card charges between here and there. In fact, there are no credit card charges at all."

"Initially he was going to Nova Scotia. Now he thinks it's better to stay out of sight where he can't be found. Which is why he's paying cash."

Alex wanted to say that if Lee was innocent he had nothing to worry about. But the reassuring words struck in his throat, since he'd had a taste of what happened when it looked as if you were guilty of murder.

"When did you speak to Lee?" he asked.

"After the announcement of the funeral."

"You called him?"

"No. He contacts me when he wants to talk."

"Well, tell him that he's created some problems for me."

"He knows that."

"And I need his signature on some documents," Sara broke in to the conversation.

Dana's eyes narrowed. "I guess that will have to wait until he feels like it's safe to come out of hiding."

"How long will that be?" Alex asked.

"Until they find out who murdered Bandy."

"Well, the police are working on it," Alex answered.

"And?" Lee's girlfriend asked, an edge in her voice.

"And they don't keep me updated, seeing as how I started off as their chief suspect."

She nodded and started to turn away. Before she could make her escape, he asked, "Are you sure it was Lee?"

"I beg your pardon?"

"Are you sure it was Lee calling you and not somebody imitating his voice?"

She stopped and considered. "Well…"

Alex waited.

"I guess I can't be absolutely sure," she murmured.

"If something's happened to Lee, then you could be in danger," he said. "Both Sara and I are being cautious."

He saw her considering that point, saw her gaze slide to Sara then back to him again.

"You might want to get out of town for a while," he said.

"Thank you for the advice," she answered stiffly.

"You're not concerned?"

"Of course I'm concerned."

"If you decide to leave, I'd appreciate a number where I can get in touch with you," he said, giving her his business card.

"I'll do that." Stuffing the card in her purse, Dana wheeled around and marched away.

Beside him, Sara said something under her breath that he probably wasn't meant to catch. "What?"

"It sounds like she came here for a business discussion, not to offer sympathy," she murmured.

"Yeah."

"So what was it she wanted us to know?"

"That Lee's in hiding because he's worried?" he answered.

"Do you believe her?"

Alex shrugged, leading her toward the car. After slipping behind the wheel, he turned his head toward her. "I've been saying thank-you a lot. I should say it to you."

"You don't have to."

He captured her hand and held it. "I want to."

He saw her nod. Because he didn't know what else to say at the moment, he focused on the narrow road ahead. Most of the cars had pulled away, but he could see Dana's Cadillac gliding toward the cemetery gates. On a hunch, he fell into line behind her, letting several cars get between them.

Sara gave him a questioning look. "Do you think she's up to something?"

"I just have a bad feeling about her."

The Cadillac, which was about a hundred yards ahead of them, turned off onto a side road.

Alex let more space fill the gap between the two vehicles, wondering if Dana would realize she was being followed.

When she turned into a restaurant parking lot, he slowed but kept going down the road.

Beside him he heard Sara gasp.

He twisted toward her. "What is it? What's wrong?"

"That's him," she croaked.

"Lee?"

"No. One of the men who was following me around. One of the militiamen," she clarified.

He stifled the impulse to slam on the brakes. "Are you sure?"

"Yes. And I know which one it was," she said. "From the pictures Hempstead showed me."

After the massacre, the chief had asked her to look at a collection of mug shots, and she'd identified some of the men who had been following her. Some were among the dead, some among the missing.

"Who is it?" Alex growled. Since the awful day he'd accompanied the police to the Fairmont Estate, he hadn't given up hope of catching his brother's murderer.

"Tripp Kenney," she answered.

The militia leader, who was one of the men who'd escaped. But so far Hempstead hadn't gotten a line on him. Apparently he'd come out of hiding. To meet Dana Eustice?

Alex found a driveway, pulled in, then had to wait impatiently for several cars to pass before he could back up and swing toward the restaurant.

Meanwhile, he started quizzing Sara. "He was in a car?"

"Yes, a silver one."

"What make?"

"Alex, I don't know an awful lot about cars."

"And you didn't get the license number?"

She made a small, distressed sound. "We were going pretty fast. All I saw was him sitting there. It was just a flash of his face, but I recognized him."

"Okay."

He reached the restaurant and took the driveway to the parking area. There were fifteen cars in the lot, none of which was the Cadillac. And nobody was sitting in any of the others—silver or not.

Alex drove around the building and tried the other entrance. But they still found no evidence of Kenney.

"Maybe I was mistaken," Sara muttered.

"We can't be sure," he told her. "If Dana knew we were following her, she could have warned him."

"You think it wasn't a coincidence. I mean, you think they were meeting each other here? And it has something to do with Lee's disappearance?"

"I don't know," Alex answered in frustration. "I should have pulled in right after her."

"Then she would have known for sure that we were on her tail."

"But we might have found something out."

"Don't beat yourself up over it," she soothed.

His only answer was a grimace.

"Maybe Ms. Eustice just ducked in here to lose us— which she did."

"Maybe," he agreed, thinking that there were too many loose ends and not enough leads in this case—whatever the case was. Lee Tillman. The attacks on Sara. Emmett Bandy. Dana Eustice. The militia massacre. Tripp Kenney. Somehow he was sure they all fit together. He just didn't know how. And he didn't know if the trunkful of clothing in Lee's attic was simply a side issue.

"What are you thinking about so hard?" Sara asked. She wasn't demanding an answer. She was simply asking, and he should have appreciated that.

She hadn't made any demands on him. She'd been giving him all the breathing space he needed, considering that they were moving around Talbot County together like Gypsies.

He sighed. "I was thinking about my trip to Baltimore."

When she remained silent, he continued, "I'm trying to locate a woman named Callie Anderson."

Again she made no comment, and he decided that maybe it might be helpful to bounce his theory off her.

"In the trunk in Lee's attic I found the letters to her."

"And you're just telling me about it now?"

"Yes."

"Okay. I guess you have your reasons."

"I wanted more information before we talked about it. Does the name Callie Anderson mean anything to you?"

"No."

"The letters were from her father asking her to come home because her mother was dying."

Sara was watching him closely.

He had reached their current abode—a motel between St. Stephens and Easton. Pulling to a stop in front of their door, he told her all about how he'd searched and finally found the old man Simmons who'd remembered the family.

Sara was focused on him with total attention as he related how Simmons thought the father had been abusive to his daughters and about their fates. Alex took a breath and went on. "Mr. Simmons had heard that the younger one, Callie, had gotten pregnant. I wonder if, after she left home, Callie took up with Lee Tillman. I was thinking, what if he got her pregnant then took the baby to St. Stephens, where he knew there was a lawyer arranging adoptions?''

He saw her turning that information over in her mind. ''Are you wondering if Lee Tillman is my father—and that's why he was so nice to me?''

''I was considering it. So I stopped in at Birth Data, Inc. I thought maybe Lee had brought the baby down there. But it turned out a woman, not a man, did it.''

''So what if he abandoned her, then regretted it and went looking for the baby later?''

''That's possible.''

''You said there was another sister. What happened to her?''

''I don't know. I'd like to find her and ask some questions.''

''Why not ask Callie?''

''Mr. Simmons heard she died, although that might not be true. But I've got my contacts in Baltimore working on locating either or both of them.''

''She died...'' Sara murmured. ''Do you think that Lee killed her?'' she asked suddenly.

''The thought crossed my mind.''

''I hope it's not true.''

''So do I. I don't want to think the old bastard was capable of murder.''

''Was?''

''I'm having trouble believing he's alive,'' Alex allowed.

''His girlfriend said she talked to him.''

''Maybe she's lying. Or maybe, like I said, somebody tricked her into thinking it was Lee.''

"But she knows him pretty well, why would she believe it?" Sara persisted.

"Because she wanted to. Because it gave her hope that he was coming back."

Sara was silent for several moments, digesting that, before she asked, "And do you think his disappearance has something to do with me?"

He answered at once because he'd already given the question considerable thought. "No. I believe you're a side issue."

She expelled a small breath. "Thanks for that, anyway."

Before he could respond, his cell phone rang.

Snatching it out of his pocket, he snapped, "Shane."

"I have some important information about Lee Tillman. Information you don't want to fall into police hands."

"Oh yeah? Who are you?"

"You don't need to know that."

"You're just a good citizen doing his duty?"

"Sure." There was a quaver in the voice. Then it grew firmer. "And I'll meet you back at the cemetery. By your brother's grave. Tonight at 9:00 p.m."

He was about to ask another question, when the phone went dead.

"What?" Sara asked.

His fingers clenched on the phone. "Somebody with information about Lee. He says that it's something I don't want the police to know."

"And?"

"He's set up a meeting tonight, by my brother's grave."

Sara sucked in a sharp breath. "That's crazy. Of course you're not going."

"Maybe I am."

"Alex, it sounds like an ambush." She dragged in a breath and let it out in a rush. "It sounds like what happened when you went down to Emmett Bandy's real estate office.''

He was thinking the same thing. He was thinking that he was being set up. He was thinking he'd be taking a damn foolish chance to meet with an anonymous phone caller. But at the same time, this case had become personal to him. Every avenue he'd pursued had led to a dead end, and maybe he had an opportunity to change that tonight.

"Send Hempstead," Sara said.

"That won't work. The guy sounded scared. If he thinks the police are involved, he'll bail out."

She folded her arms across her chest. "If you won't call Hempstead, I will."

"No. The guy will run if you do. Let me set it up so it looks like I'm being a patsy again. Only this time I'll be prepared. This time I'll make it work out for me."

Her eyes turned fierce. "What are you trying to prove?"

"Nothing."

"Then you must have a death wish!"

"No," he answered automatically.

"If you say so," she muttered, then deliberately turned her head away.

His features set in grim lines, he sat staring through the windshield. Somewhere in a small corner of his mind, he knew he wasn't exactly operating rationally. Maybe he *was* being self-destructive. He'd lost the perspective to figure that out.

ALEX SPENT the rest of the day getting ready—and trying to talk Sara out of going with him to the cemetery. But she wouldn't listen. If he was going, so was she. When he objected, she repeated her threat to call Hempstead and threw in the state police for good measure. He thought about tying her up so she couldn't follow him, but discarded the idea as impractical. Which was why she was in the back seat of the car, ducking low so she wouldn't be seen, as he made his way up the narrow lane where he'd parked that morning.

Only now it was almost pitch-black, the moon dancing in and out from behind wispy clouds.

A cemetery wasn't his favorite place during the day. At night it conjured up images of malevolent spirits rising up from behind marble monuments to wreak vengeance on the living.

What about Billy's spirit? he wondered. Had his brother found the peace in death that had eluded him in life? Or was he suffering the tortures of the damned? Alex had decided long ago that he didn't believe in hell. Now he found himself hoping that his brother wasn't there. Or maybe his offenses had only been bad enough to get him into purgatory. After all, he hadn't killed anyone. Not that Alex knew about, anyway. At the militia compound, he hadn't even drawn his weapon before he was shot.

Alex had come to the cemetery in the afternoon to check out the area and make sure he could find the meeting place after dark without a flashlight. After the service, there had been a huge pile of dirt beside the grave, covered discreetly with a carpet of fake green grass. By the afternoon, it was gone, the earth tamped into the new rectangular hole. Too bad, Alex thought. He could have hidden on top of the casket and given his informant a heart attack when he jumped out.

The image cheered him somewhat. Then he considered that he might have come here to meet nobody at all.

Because there was one other possibility he'd been forced to consider: that the phone call this afternoon was part of a hoax, perpetrated by someone who wanted to rub in his brother's murder—or rub in the fact that he wasn't getting anywhere with the Lee Tillman case.

It had been raw and cold here in the morning. Now the wind had a cutting edge as it whipped past gravestones and pierced Alex's exposed skin.

Pulling up the collar of his coat, he ducked his head and made for a large reddish granite tombstone.

He never reached it. As he turned toward his right, a crack like thunder suddenly split the air, and he felt a bullet slam into his chest.

Chapter Fourteen

He heard gravel crunch, heard running feet. Then Sara's voice filtered past the pain in his chest. Grimly he struggled to stand but couldn't manage it, and he wondered if a high-powered projectile had penetrated the bulletproof vest he was wearing and torn apart his flesh. As he analyzed the pain, he realized the shield had done its work and captured the bullet. But the impact had still slammed into him like a steel wrecking ball.

"Drop your gun and raise your hands, you bastard!" Sara shouted.

Someone—a man—answered the order with a curse. His weapon landed on the ground with a thump.

Fighting pain, Alex drew in a ragged breath as he heaved himself up and staggered forward. He found Sara holding the Glock he'd given her—two hands on the gun like a TV cop. She was facing a man who stood with his back against a tombstone.

"It's Tripp Kenney," she informed him.

The militia leader. Well, well.

The man stared at him, wide-eyed. "But I shot you in the chest," he breathed. "Why aren't you dead?"

"Bulletproof vest," Alex spat out, still struggling to

stand still. If Kenney tried anything, he wasn't going to be much help to Sara. "Move away from the grave marker."

The man took a step forward. As Sara covered Kenney, Alex came up behind him and cuffed his hands, the way Hempstead had cuffed him days before.

Turning to her, he growled, "I told you to stay in the car."

She stared at him with an "I told you so" look, but she only said, "If I had, he would have gotten away."

Alex acknowledged the comment with a small huff that made Sara's anxious gaze shoot to his face.

"Are you all right?" she asked urgently.

"I'll live." He shined his flashlight on the ground and spotted the gun that Kenney had dropped. A .380 Walther. Lucky for him, he thought. Something bigger and he might be in the hospital right now, despite the vest.

He started to reach for the gun, then checked himself. He'd bag the evidence later, so he didn't screw up the prints.

Alex turned toward the man who had clearly tried to kill him. "Sit down so we can talk," he said. Putting a hand on the man's shoulder, he pressed him down so that he was sitting on the grave. The militia leader's features hardened. But Alex suspected he was probably shaking inside.

"So now we're going to have the chat you promised me when you called me earlier. It was you who called, right?"

"Yeah, it was me."

"First you killed my brother. Then you tried to get me," he spat out. "Why?"

"I didn't kill your brother."

"Who did?"

"A militiaman—Al Bigelow. But he got drilled by another one of our soldiers, Curt Morgan, so it's a moot point.''

"Who started the shooting?''

"Not me. You've got to believe that. I had an insurrection on my hands.''

"You mean, your militia turned into a mob?'' Alex asked with a snort.

"It was brewing for a long time. I thought I could control them, but I was wrong. There was a disagreement about going after you the other day.''

"Regarding the dog and the firefight?''

He nodded. "The discussion got pretty heated. Some guys were with me, some thought I'd made a bad mistake—drawing unwanted attention to us.'' He grimaced. "Somebody drew a gun and fired. Somebody fired back. And then there was no stopping it.''

"Like when you shot Emmett Bandy?'' Alex growled.

"I didn't do him!''

"Sure.'' Alex lowered his face toward the man. "And you didn't shoot at me just now?''

"That was different. I needed the money. After the mess at the compound, I needed to get out of here, start over fresh with a new identity. I'm the only guy who got out of there alive, who's still hanging around here. Everyone else has taken off. And I've got to make tracks too.''

"You're saying somebody paid you to get rid of me? Who?''

The man's lips clamped shut. "I can't tell you.''

"Oh yeah?'' Alex wanted to plow his fist into the man's face. Somehow he stopped himself.

But Kenney must have seen the anger in his eyes. Frantically, he tried to push himself away. Alex clamped a hand on his shoulder.

"Take it easy," he said, the advice intended as much for himself as Kenney. "You're not going anywhere."

The militiaman's eyes darted from side to side, but he stayed where he was as Alex pulled out the Sig he'd gotten back from the police and trained it on him. With his other hand, he extracted his cell phone and gave it to Sara. "Call 911," he said, "and tell them we're at Green Meadow Cemetery. Tell them we have a shooting suspect in custody."

"No!" Kenney bellowed.

"Why not?"

"It's not me you want. It's—"

Before he could finish the sentence, a shot rang out.

Alex grabbed Sara and threw her to the ground, just as another shot whizzed over his head.

From the sound of it, the bullet had come from a high-powered rifle, he thought with one part of his mind as he covered Sara's body with his own. Pressing her to the cold ground, he prayed that his dark coat made them less of a target.

"Are you all right?" he asked urgently.

"Yes," she gasped. "I can't believe this. Someone else shot at us. Someone else is here."

"Yeah. Stay down," he answered, cursing himself again. He'd been prepared to meet a possible assassin tonight. He hadn't considered that somebody else was coming along to make sure that Tripp Kenney kept his mouth shut.

For several moments, he remained where he was, but there was no more gunfire. Raising himself to a crouch, Alex half dragged, half carried Sara behind a nearby grave marker, his chest on fire from the effort.

Cautiously he raised his head and looked around. He

saw Kenney sprawled against the white marble. Already dead.

"Stay down," he told Sara as he moved off in the direction from which the shot had come. "And call the cops."

Behind him he could hear Sara making the call to 911. He'd used the police as a threat when he'd handed her the phone earlier. Now...now they needed the law. The rational part of his brain knew that. They couldn't leave Kenney's body in the cemetery and run.

But another part of his mind was silently screaming, *No. Not again. Please, God, not again.*

He found no one else on the scene. The shooter had fled.

Carefully he replaced his gun in its holster. As he came back to Billy's grave, he unbuckled the belt and set the whole thing on the ground.

"Put your gun down," he said to Sara, keeping his voice flat and even. She followed his lead, then moved to his side, and he slung his arm around her, holding her close.

"What's going to happen when the police get here?" she whispered.

"It's going to be okay," he said, still making an effort to keep his voice steady. "But they're going to have to consider us suspects. At least initially. They're going to prone us."

"What?"

"They're going to make us lie down on the ground and cuff us," he muttered. "When they see what's happened here, they have to."

"But we *called* them," she protested.

"Yeah. But they're not going to risk their lives on our being nice guys."

She made a small, distressed sound, and he pulled her around to face him, held her tighter.

He felt as if he were waiting centuries for a ten-ton block of granite to fall on him. And at the same time, it seemed no more than the blink of an eye before a couple of patrol cars pulled up on the road.

Lord, he'd been stupid again, he thought. Stupid for agreeing to this secret meeting. He should have at least called Hempstead and told him what he was doing.

"Follow my lead," he said, raising his hands as the cops exited their cruiser.

Jaw clenched, Sara did the same. It didn't make him feel any better that he recognized the two uniforms who emerged from the first car. They were the same guys, Glenn and Taubman, who had hauled him in after the chief picked him up for the shooting at Emmett Bandy's office.

"We're unarmed," he said. "We were meeting Tripp Kenney, the militia leader. Kenney shot at me. Then somebody else shot him. He's dead." He jerked his head toward the body propped against the tombstone.

The two officers followed his gaze, then drew their weapons.

Sara gasped.

"Steady," he whispered.

"Down on the ground," Taubman ordered.

"Do it," he told Sara.

They both went down. At least the grass was thick and springy, he thought as Taubman snapped cuffs on his wrists, then patted him down.

"Bulletproof vest?"

"Yeah," he answered. "You'll find the bullet where Kenney shot me. And holes in my clothing to match. Lucky for me, he wasn't carrying a cannon."

Still, when the uniform helped him to his feet again, he couldn't hold back a wince.

"You hurt?" the cop asked.

"I'll live."

He stayed close to Sara, who was saying, in a high strained voice, "Kenney asked Alex to meet him here, then he shot at Alex. I, uh, I got the drop on him. Then Alex handcuffed him so he couldn't get away."

He took up the narrative. "Kenney was about to tell us who sent him here, when somebody made sure he wasn't going to spill the beans. You'll find powder burns on his hands. His weapon's over there on the ground. It will match the bullet in my vest." He sighed. "My gun hasn't been fired. It's also on the ground, along with Sara's, which also hasn't been fired. Is this starting to sound familiar?"

"Yeah."

"Only, this time, he has a witness," Sara said. "I saw everything. Well, I didn't see who fired at us while we were talking to Kenney."

"Uh-huh." Glenn cleared his throat. "We do have to take you in for questioning."

Alex sighed. "Of course. I'm sure Dan Cassidy will love coming down from Baltimore again." Raising his chin, he looked from Glenn to Taubman. "And this time, since I came to interview a witness who asked to set up this meeting, I have a tape recorder with me. So there's no question about what happened. The recorder is in my right coat pocket. You can reach inside and get it, and turn off the tape. Or you can arrest me for recording a conversation without the other party's knowledge. But I don't think Kenney's going to object."

Glenn retrieved the recorder. "Let's go," he said.

History repeated itself with another ride in the back of

a police car, only this time Sara was beside him. In a kind of warped way, Alex was glad she was there, glad that she turned in her seat and pressed her face against his shoulder. Stroking her with his lips, talking to her in a low, soothing voice helped him calm his own jumping nerves during the ride.

When he got to the state police barracks, he was forced to make a decision. They could wait in a holding cell for Dan Cassidy to come down from Baltimore, or he could let them start interviewing him and Sara.

"I'd like to get this over with," he told Sara.

"Will they let us stay together?" she asked.

"No. They want to hear our stories separately. Can you handle that?"

"Yes," she answered, but he could see she didn't love the idea.

TO HIS VAST RELIEF they were out of the state police barracks just three hours after they'd entered. They even had an offer of police protection, since somebody had clearly shot Kenney in front of them, and they were the only witnesses.

Alex wasn't prepared to have his activities monitored, although he'd tried to get Sara to accept the offer. Or to get out of the state. But she was still with him when the officers who had picked them up at the cemetery gave them a ride back to the SUV.

She was silent the whole way back. Silent as they stood beside the truck waiting for the police cruiser to pull away. And he wondered what she was thinking. Was she blaming him?

As soon as he unlocked the doors and they climbed inside, she turned wordlessly toward him. When she reached for him, he reached back, folding her into his arms.

"Alex, I was so scared," she murmured. "I was afraid they were going to think we did it. And then when they separated us, I thought I was going to lose it."

"You did great."

"I know it was only a little taste of what you got when they arrested you last time. But it scared me spitless, because I kept thinking that just because you're innocent doesn't mean you don't get charged with murder."

His hands soothed over her back. Lord, it felt so good to hold her. So right. And despite all the warnings he'd given himself, all the uncertainty, he didn't have the strength to resist the need for her.

Since the last time they'd made love, they'd been carefully moving around each other, as if each of them wasn't burning for the other. Now she lifted her face to his, and he brought his mouth down to hers for a long, deep kiss that left them both breathing raggedly.

"I should keep my hands off you," he muttered. "We have to get out of here."

"But I *want* your hands on me. I need them on me!" To reinforce the point, she found one of his hands and dragged it under her coat, cupping it around her breast. He caressed her softness, found his fingers drawn to her hardened nipple.

Once he started, he simply couldn't find the strength to stop. She moved against him, making a frustrated, whimpering sound that turned the blood in his veins molten.

"Alex, Alex, I need you now," she gasped, sounding as crazed as he felt. "Oh Lord, I wish I'd worn a skirt."

He wanted to keep kissing her, touching her, but the frantic sound of her voice brought back a measure of sanity.

His rumbling curse made her head jerk up, her eyes searching his.

"If I were trying to set up another ambush, I couldn't do a better job than this," he growled.

"Whoever shot Kenney is long gone," she said in a steady voice.

"Maybe. But that's no excuse for putting you in danger. And I don't think either one of us would like it much if the cops come back to check on us." He saw that comment hit the mark.

"Put your seat belt on," he growled. "There's a seat belt law in Maryland."

He drove her back to their current motel, where they stayed long enough to pack up. Then he made absolutely sure they weren't being followed before driving to another anonymous lodging place on the opposite side of town.

He was scanning the parking lot when she emerged from the bathroom wearing an oversize T-shirt instead of a nightgown. He saw her hesitate in the doorway.

"Are you coming to bed?" she asked in a low voice.

"I have work to do."

He watched her hands clench and unclench at her sides. Then she crossed the room and slipped her arms around him, pressing her cheek to his shoulder. He felt her draw in a breath and let it out before she said, "Are you still trying to pretend that the two of us don't care deeply about each other?"

"I should."

"But you've given it up?"

He felt his heart pounding in his chest. Probably she could feel it, too. He couldn't form an answer, not with words. But when her arms tightened around him, he gathered her close.

"I don't want to waste time arguing with you," she murmured.

"Yeah, well, if you're thinking of wasting time in some more pleasant way, I'm afraid I've got to disappoint you. I wasn't kidding about needing to work. I've got to get back online and check my messages. I'm expecting some information from Randolph Security." He sucked in a breath, then let it out in a rush. "Sara, we have to deal with the mess we're in before we can talk about…our relationship."

She raised her head and looked at him, and he was pretty sure she knew he was manufacturing excuses.

But she didn't call him on it. Instead, she said, "I understand," and stepped away.

He had to flatten his hands against his sides to stop himself from reaching for her once more. Her backing off was the single most effective thing she could do to get his full attention. Instead, he deliberately turned away and reached for the laptop computer while she climbed into bed.

He could feel her watching him as he sat down at the desk, and he wanted to close up the machine, lie down beside her and gather her to him. Keeping his gaze fixed on the screen, he got into his mail system and found a message from Randolph Security.

He'd been too busy to go back to Baltimore, so he'd asked for information on Lacy and Callie Anderson, the sisters who had been abused by their father. As it turned out, the request had been handed over to the Light Street Detective Agency, which worked closely with Randolph. Bree Brennan, the Light Street staffer who did most of the research work, had handled the request.

He found confirmation that Callie Anderson was dead.

And some information about her sister Lacy that made his eyes widen in shock.

He sat there for a long time, going through the information from Bree, trying to rearrange his thinking.

He'd been almost sure that Lee Tillman was dead. Now he was wondering again if the man had decided to pull a disappearing act.

Maybe he'd be able to figure it out after another trip to The Refuge. But before he went to Tillman's, he had another important stop to make.

Some time after two in the morning, he did take off his shirt and jeans and lie down on the double bed. Almost immediately Sara moved toward him in her sleep.

He settled against her, wondering what the hell he was going to tell her about Lacy Anderson. There had been so many secrets between them. Now he was carrying around another—something Sara should know. But he couldn't tell her—not until he cleared it with Lee. If Lee was still alive.

He slept better than he'd expected, and when he woke he felt refreshed. Maybe because since he'd hooked up with Sara he hadn't been awakened by one of his nightmares.

Just before first light, he eased out of bed, took a quick shower, then opened Sara's purse and quietly took out her keys. Carefully he removed the one he'd watched her use on Lee Tillman's front door. After replacing the rest of the keys, he crossed the room and bent over Sara, stroking her cheek until her eyes fluttered open and focused on him.

"I'm going out," he said.

"Where?"

"To the cemetery to look around," he said, telling her part of his plans. "Go back to sleep."

"Um…"

She closed her eyes again, and he slipped out of the room, carefully locking the door behind him.

Back to the scene of the crime, he thought as he pulled through the gates of Green Meadow Cemetery and drove up the road, passing the spot where he and Sara had grabbed each other and held on for dear life, until he'd called a halt.

The wild, possessive flood of feelings that had engulfed him then came sweeping back. He had needed Sara more than he had ever needed anyone in his life, and the realization was enough to make his mouth go dry. He'd told her last night that they had to solve the Lee Tillman case before they could focus on their relationship. What he should have said was that he was scared spitless to think in relationship terms because his mind kept asking the question "What if Sara turned out to be like Cindy?"

Cindy had been passionate. Cindy had said she loved him. And then she'd turned around and brought another man to their marriage bed.

Momentarily light-headed, he clamped his hands around the steering wheel, trying to anchor himself.

As he did, he deliberately started coming up with all the ways that Sara was different from Cindy. Cindy had never pretended to need anyone. She'd been self-possessed and independent, right from the first.

He'd thought he liked those qualities. They'd turned out to mean she didn't need him.

But Sara...Sara had called him when Billy and his partner were after her. She'd thought of him before any other source of rescue. And that wasn't all. She hadn't just reached out to him for help. She'd been there for him, too. Like when she'd gone upstairs to get the rifle or when she rushed in and had gotten the drop on Tripp Kenney.

She'd trusted him to save her life. Then she'd returned

the favor and risked her life to save him. Both of those things fairly took his breath away when he considered them separately and together.

The new insights warmed him.

Until they led him to other thoughts. In the silence of the cemetery, sitting only a few yards from his brother's grave, he was struck by a painful realization. He'd been acting like a fool. Sara had accused him of being self-destructive. So had Dan, for that matter. And maybe they were both right.

He'd been in pain over the failure of his marriage and that had given him a certain dangerous attitude about his own safety. He hadn't cared if he'd taken risks. Actually, to be brutally honest, he'd gone searching for risky solutions to problems. Maybe he'd even been secretly hoping that somebody would kill him. And it wouldn't be his fault.

He died with his boots on, folks. In the line of duty.

Then he'd met Sara. And getting involved with her had only made things worse. He'd been terrified to admit his feelings for her. Terrified to confront his vulnerability.

So his behavior had gotten more risky, more reckless. And the risk hadn't been only to himself. He'd dragged Sara into the danger zone with him.

A deep, guttural sound tore through his chest. Sara. He'd been risking Sara's life because of his own doubts. Both of them could have gotten killed here last night when that sniper had started shooting. And whatever happened between them, putting her in jeopardy was the worst mistake he'd made in a long line of recent mistakes.

So what to do about it?

His hands tightened into fists. Well, for starters he had to face his own shortcomings and admit that he wasn't a one-man vigilante squad. He had to accept help from somebody.

He was going to call Hempstead. After he took care of a couple more items on his own.

When his surroundings finally registered on his consciousness again, he realized it was fully light. He'd better get on with his search before the cops showed up and he got charged with impeding a police investigation.

He walked back to the spot where he'd been standing when Kenney had taken the bullet. He made a visual inspection of the area from outside the yellow police tape. Then he considered where the shooter would have been.

There were several reasons why he thought the bullet had come from a high-powered rifle. The sound was one clue. Then there was the accuracy of the shot and the amount of damage the slug had done to the militia leader's chest.

And finally, there was the getaway. Whoever had shot Kenney had been far enough from the kill to make an easy escape into the darkness.

Which meant he'd been using a telescopic lens. Specifically a nightscope.

Not so long ago, a nightscope would have been expensive. Now anyone could buy a right nice one in almost any neo-Nazi Survivalist or gun enthusiast catalog for about three hundred dollars. And it could be mounted on any long gun.

He thought about the distance, then walked rapidly to the part of the cemetery where he figured the shooter might have been. He wasn't sure what he was looking for. Anything, really. A cigarette butt, a chewing-gum wrapper, a beer bottle. Something that might provide DNA evidence.

Twenty minutes after he'd started searching, he hit pay dirt. A glint of sunlight off metal led him to a small brass cylinder with a swirly rainbow-colored ring around the mouth.

Carefully, he used a small stick to pick it up.

It was a shell casing. In the dark and in his haste to get away, the killer had failed to retrieve it after it had been ejected from his rifle.

Looking at it, Alex felt a chill run down his spine. It wasn't just any shell casing. It was from a very recognizable gun, a .22 Hornet. Although it was a great rifle for hunting or assassinations, there weren't very many of them around. It had good ballistics, good range for a small caliber, almost no recoil. It was inherently accurate. Yet somehow it had never caught on with the great gun-owning public.

However, Alex knew who owned one.

Chapter Fifteen

Lee Tillman owned a .22 Hornet. Alex had seen it in his gun cabinet and commented on it. And the man, in his blustering macho way, had given him a twenty-minute recitation on its virtues.

Alex carefully set the casing down where he'd found it. He'd told the police he thought the weapon that had killed Kenney had been a high-powered rifle, so hopefully they'd search the same area he had. They'd find the calling card, they'd start checking gun shops and they'd find out who had bought Hornet shells.

So was Lee alive? And had he killed Bandy after all— and then Tripp Kenney? Or had the same person who'd killed Lee also killed the other two?

Alex walked rapidly back to his car. When he'd set out this morning, he'd had a good reason to go to Lee's house. Now he had another one—to see if by some chance the Hornet was still in the gun cabinet.

His mind was working rapidly as he climbed into the SUV and started toward The Refuge. If the gun was missing and the killer wasn't Lee, then it was most likely somebody with access to the house.

Lewis Farmer, the handyman, was a prime candidate. He worked for Lee, and he'd come snooping around on the same day that Alex and Sara had been checking out the attic. Apparently, he didn't have a key to the house. But Lee could have let him in on the fatal morning. After killing Lee, Lewis could have taken his victim's rifle.

What was his motive, though? Maybe robbery, since he seemed chronically short of money. Or maybe Lee had caught him at something and he'd killed in haste. Lewis had always been a hothead—which was why it was good that he hadn't had a gun in his hand back in high school.

But was Lewis capable of planning several subsequent murders and of framing Alex for one of them? And was he working with the militia to go after Sara?

That seemed less likely. So, although Alex couldn't dismiss him as a suspect, he could come up with a more likely possibility. Which meant that he might be able to trap his suspect into a taped confession. However, this time he was going to play by the rules. He was going to ask for Hempstead's help. But he needed information to set in front of the chief—information he could only get from Lee's house.

Again he came up along the river, making sure he wasn't being observed. Again he slipped on latex gloves, then used the key that he'd taken from Sara's purse, wondering if he could slip it back before she noticed.

His first stop was the gun cabinet. The Hornet was missing, and if he recalled correctly, so were several other weapons. Like maybe the .22 handgun that had shot Emmett Bandy.

Interesting, he thought as he turned away and started for the stairs, heading for Lee's bathroom. Opening the medicine cabinet, he found several bottles of prescription drugs. He wasn't surprised to read the label on one of them. Actually, the information confirmed what Bree Brennan had told him in her e-mail.

He stood staring into space for several moments. Then he replaced the bottle where he'd found it. It seemed unlikely that Lee would have gone off without this stuff. But maybe he had a spare. Maybe he'd gotten a whole new prescription before he'd gone on vacation.

He made one more stop before he left the house. The private gallery. Stepping inside the door, he looked at the works of art, seeing them with new eyes. Leda and the Swan. The two lesbian lovers. The woman with her hands bound to the headboard. He'd thought they were kinky when he'd seen them earlier. Now he realized that they confirmed what he'd learned about Lee Tillman last night.

One picture was still missing. One picture that might be a significant clue to Lee's disappearance. What was it? he wondered.

Alex was tempted to nose around the house some more, but knew it was better not to press his luck. So he slipped outside again, locking the door behind himself. Back in his car, he phoned Hempstead's house.

"Can you meet me for breakfast?" he asked.

"Is this a social call? Or do we have some business?"

"Business," Alex answered.

"Okay. How about the doughnut shop on the south edge of town? I can be there in fifteen minutes."

Alex agreed, thinking that the man would probably be better off with skim milk and oatmeal. But he didn't voice the observation.

When he slid into the back booth across from the chief, however, and saw the strained expression on his face, he couldn't hold back a quick question. "Are you feeling okay?"

"I've got a little indigestion. Maybe I'd better skip the doughnuts."

The waitress came, and Alex ordered coffee. The chief

asked for a mug of tea, which gained a raised eyebrow from the waitress. Tea apparently wasn't his usual.

"How about telling me why you called this meeting," he said when they were alone again.

"I'd like you to help me trap a killer."

"You mean this time you're letting me in on your plans?" Hempstead asked, a wry note in his voice. "I mean instead of rushing off to get yourself arrested or shot at."

Alex shifted in his seat. He wouldn't have put it quite that way, but he understood where the chief was coming from. "Yes."

"Why?" Hempstead pressed.

Alex sighed. "I can see I've been going about this wrong. Don't rub it in, okay."

"I'm glad to hear that insight. I was worried about you, son."

"I think I've got my priorities straight now."

"You mean you're not going to break that girl's heart after all?"

Alex swallowed, unable to answer. "Maybe we'd better talk about Lee Tillman."

Hempstead gave him a considering look. "Okay." As Alex began to explain what he'd found out, the information brought a shocked expression to the chief's face.

"You're sure?" he said.

"Positive. My researcher at the Light Street Detective Agency has traced him back to the year he appeared in St. Stephens, and further back still—to his old identity."

Hempstead nodded slowly, still apparently grappling with the shocking revelation.

The tea and coffee arrived. Alex took a sip from his cup. Then he began outlining his plan. Hempstead made some suggestions, and they agreed to talk again in a couple of hours, after Alex had set things up.

Instead of heading back to the motel, Alex drove to the well-kept Victorian house where Dana Eustice lived.

Pulling up in front, he sat studying the facade for several moments, then climbed out and strode up the walk.

When he rang the bell, there was no answer, but he could hear pounding rock music from somewhere inside. Classic rock.

It wasn't what he would have expected.

He had to ring several times, then knock loudly on the door before the lady of the house appeared. She was wearing a gold leotard and gold tights. Her hair was pulled back into a ponytail, and a fine sheen of perspiration coated her skin. In the formfitting exercise outfit, her figure looked very feminine. But without makeup, her face showed more signs of age than he'd seen before. Or perhaps she was reacting to stress. Whatever had happened to Lee, she had to be concerned about him.

"I was doing my morning workout," she said.

"Yes. Can I come in for a minute?"

"It's a little early for visitors."

"This is important."

She made a face, then stepped aside. He followed her into a square entryway with an antique hall rack and stained-glass ceiling fixture, then down a hall into a well-equipped modern kitchen.

Turning to confront him, she folded her arms across her chest. "Well?"

"I need to speak to Lee," he said.

"I think Lee's made it clear that he's not available."

"It might be in his best interest to see me."

Her chin jutted out slightly. "Why?"

On the way to Dana's house, he'd mulled over several ways to play this scene. Now he made a quick decision.

"I've been digging into Lee's background. I know…" he said, letting the sentence trail off.

"About what?" she snapped.

"About his sexual-reassignment surgery."

Dana wasn't able to keep a look of dismay from washing across her face. "No," she breathed. "Nobody knows."

"I'm afraid I do. Lee Tillman was born Lacy Anderson. Twenty-eight years ago, she went to a clinic in Amsterdam and had a series of operations that changed her from a woman into a man."

Dana opened her mouth and closed it again.

"You've been Lee's girlfriend for more than twenty years. Don't tell me you didn't know about it." He pressed on, aware that he was out of bounds yet needing to wring a reaction from this woman. "It must have made some difference in your sexual relationship."

"That's none of your business."

"Maybe not. But I think you aren't Lee's only sexual partner. I think he's into some pretty kinky stuff, and his sexual practices have left him open for blackmail."

Her head jerked up. "I won't discuss this with you."

"You'd better discuss it with him. He hired me to find out who was threatening him. He left out quite a few suspects, but I've figured out the person threatening him may well be one of his sexual contacts."

Her jaw tightened. "I'm the only sexual contact that means anything to him. He doesn't get naked with anybody else. Only with me. The rest of them are…just because he has a strong sexual appetite. And it turns him on to watch other people."

The pictures had given Alex a pretty good idea of what

Lee liked to watch. Instead of commenting, he asked, "If Lee's away, why did he leave his supply of male hormone pills at home?"

"Because he's got more than one bottle of the stuff," she snapped. "And I won't allow you to go any further with this line of questioning. Lee had his reasons for changing his sex. But discussing them with you would be betraying his confidence."

"His father abused Lacy," Alex said. "Abused Lacy and her sister, Callie. Callie ran away from home, hooked up with a guy who was too much like her dad and got pregnant. She died, and Lacy placed the baby for adoption. Then she went off to Amsterdam."

Dana didn't deny the information. In a tight voice, she asked, "How do you know all that? Lee hid his background very well."

"I have my sources. One of them is the man who adopted Callie's child. He's been digging into his daughter's background, and that's led him to Lee."

Dana shook her head. "No."

"I don't think the man has the whole thing figured out. But somebody else has. This is the computer age, remember? It's a lot harder to hide secrets than it was twenty years ago." Lying with a straight face, he continued, "I've gotten a half-million-dollar blackmail demand, and it's not from the adoptive father. Somebody else has figured out who Lee is. I think your only choice is to set up a meeting between me and Lee so we can figure out what to do. I'll be back this evening at nine. Tell Lee he'd better be here."

"He may not want to come. I don't tell him what to do. You must know by now that he makes his own decisions."

"Not this time. I'll call you later to work out the details."

"What if Lee can't get back here in time?"

"He'd better."

Without giving her time to reply, he turned and strode out of the room, knowing Clark Hempstead would be very interested in how the discussion had gone.

SARA SAT in the motel-room chair watching Alex get ready for his evening meeting. Ever since he'd come back and explained what he had in mind, she'd felt like a giant fist was squeezing her chest. She didn't want him to put himself in danger. Not again. But he'd given her that hard-jawed look of his and insisted that everything was under control, because this time Chief Hempstead was his backup.

The look wasn't just from his determination to go through with his risky scheme. She'd learned to read Alex Shane over the past few days, and she knew that there was something else going on besides the meeting. Something he deliberately wasn't telling her. And she was planning to find it out.

"I'll be back in a couple of hours," he told her.

Not trusting herself to speak, she only nodded. Quickly she crossed the room. Taking him in her arms, she closed her eyes and held him tightly for several heartbeats. There was so much she wanted to say to him, starting with a plea that he come clean with her. But she couldn't do it now. Not when he needed to focus on a confrontation.

So she stepped away from him, then sat back down to give him a head start before she went after him.

It helped that she'd listened to his phone conversations with Chief Hempstead. She knew exactly what they had planned. And she didn't have to follow Alex. She could catch up with him after he reached Dana Eustice's house.

Five minutes later, she climbed into her car and headed into St. Stephens.

IT WAS FULLY DARK when Alex drove slowly past the neat white Victorian house that he'd visited early that morning, noting the light shining through the closed blinds in the living room. Was Lee in there? Or was it his killer?

Pulling around the corner, he saw a gray windowless van parked at the curb. He knew Clark Hempstead was inside. Without approaching the vehicle, he parked and spoke into the darkness of his SUV. "If you're reading me, flash your lights."

The lights on the van flashed briefly.

Alex nodded to himself. "Okay, I'm going in," he said, climbing out and starting up the alley, thinking it was too bad Hempstead couldn't send a verbal acknowledgment. But the transmission went only one way.

Listening to the crunch of his footsteps on the gravel surface, he concentrated on looking as if his heart wasn't threatening to pound its way through the wall of his chest. He wasn't worried about getting killed, he assured himself. He was simply on edge because he didn't know whom he was going to meet.

He didn't want it to be Lee. But in many ways, the alternative was worse.

He'd talked to Dana again, setting up the meeting. And as they'd arranged, the back door was open. Stepping inside, he made his way through the kitchen and down a short hall to the living room.

Ms. Eustice was waiting for him, sitting in a chintz-covered wingback chair, wearing a flowing green and gold caftan.

"Did you give Lee my message about the blackmail scheme?" Alex asked.

"Yes. Unfortunately, he couldn't be here."

Alex knew that was a damn lie. No way would Lee Tillman ignore a demand for half a million dollars.

"He's not worried about the whole world discovering who he is?"

"It won't matter because he's not coming back."

"You mean because you killed him?" Alex asked in a conversational voice. "And then you killed Emmett Bandy and Tripp Kenney?"

Dana gave him a narrow-eyed look, then pulled a small revolver from the folds of her caftan and trained it on Alex. "Right. I killed them, and you're next," she said in a low voice.

"You admit it?"

"Why not? You're not going to tell anyone."

Except Clark Hempstead, Alex thought, wondering how long it was going to be before the chief came bursting through the door.

AS SARA DROVE slowly down the block, she saw the gray van. Saw Alex's car parked in back of it. Saw something was badly wrong.

The driver's door of the van was open, and Chief Hempstead was lying on the ground, gasping for breath, his face contorted with pain.

She pulled to the curb and slammed on her brakes. In seconds, she was down on her knees beside the chief, a strange background buzzing in her ears. "What? What's wrong."

"My heart," he gasped. "I called 911 and called for backup."

As he spoke, she suddenly realized then that the buzzing sound was coming from a small box on the ground beside the chief. It was a receiver, no doubt attached to a transmitter Alex was wearing. Quickly, she turned up the sound so she could hear better.

Alex was saying, "You imitated Lee's voice to make me think he was still alive."

"Yes. I'm very good at voices," a woman replied. It was Dana Eustice. "My theater training, you know."

"Why did you kill him?"

The question riveted Sara's attention.

"Why should I tell you?" Dana asked.

"Because I've worked hard for the answers."

"A lot of good they're going to do you." She sighed. "All right. Lee was mine. He used to like inviting other people in for performances. Kinky performances, like you said. But he didn't join in the action. He was into scenes where he directed the actors and watched the action."

"Scenes like in his picture gallery?"

"Yes, like that. I could deal with his diversions, but then he started going after that sweet little thing—Sara Delaney. Buying her stuff, paying her college tuition, giving her jobs that paid ridiculous amounts of money. I wasn't going to lose him to her. Not after all these years."

"That's crap! Sara was Lee's niece. His dead sister's girl."

"No!"

"Oh, yes. That's part of what I found out when I started digging into Lee's background."

Sara was so stunned that she couldn't move. She'd thought Lee Tillman might be her father, but it turned out he was her uncle? Dana Eustice had killed him. Now she was going to kill Alex, she realized, pulling herself together.

"I've got to go to Alex," she whispered.

"No…dangerous," Chief Hempstead said from the ground. "Backup…here soon."

"He's in danger now!"

When Hempstead saw the determination in her eyes, he heaved a pained sigh. "Take my gun."

With the gun in one hand and the receiver in the other, Sara started running up the alley.

She thought she heard Hempstead call out something, but she ignored him and kept running. The voices from the box stayed with her as the conversation inside the house continued.

"Where did Lee get the money for his sex-change operation?" Alex was saying. "The operation that transformed Lacy Anderson into Lee Tillman."

Sara almost dropped the speaker box. Sex change operation?

"Lacy lived through years of abuse. She swore that men would never get the better of her again. She was going to beat them at their own game. So she found a rich old man to keep her, and she helped him along to his grave, shall we say. Then she took the guy's money and went off to that clinic in Amsterdam that you found out about. Damn you! Why couldn't you just leave it alone?"

"Because Lee was paying me to protect him. Too bad he never told you who adopted Callie's baby after Lacy brought her down to St. Stephens. Then you would have known Sara Delaney was his niece."

"No. I won't believe that!"

"Right, of course you don't want to believe. You killed Lee because you thought he was sweet on Sara. Maybe if I hadn't been stopped on the road by that work crew, I would have caught you dragging his body out of the house. So why don't you tell me what you did with him after you wrapped him in his rug and carted him downstairs."

"You'll never find him! He's at the bottom of the bay in an old trunk. I did him a favor. The world will never

know his secret. I even got rid of the painting in his gallery
that might have given him away.''

''What painting was that?''

''The man and the woman in bed making love. The man
and the woman with the same face. Like identical twins.''

''So why did you do Bandy and Kenney? Were you
doing them a favor, too?''

''Kenney was working for me. Going after Sara.''

''But you kept it up after Lee was dead. Why?''

''I was punishing the bitch. She's the one responsible
for Lee's death.''

Sara gasped. By what twisted logic, she wondered, had
Dana come to that conclusion?

''And Bandy?'' Alex was saying.

''Lee hated him. His death was no loss. I figured I could
get you off the investigation by doing him.''

''So you imitated his voice and Lee's voice on my answering machine?''

''You have it all figured out, don't you? But it's not
going to do you any good.''

Sara had reached the house. God, now what? Dana was
in there holding a gun on Alex. He must be waiting for
Hempstead to come charging in—but Hempstead was lying out on the ground beside his van.

So it was up to her.

Quietly Sara opened the door she knew had been left
unlocked for Alex and stepped into an empty kitchen.
Knowing she had to get Dana's attention away from Alex,
she twisted the volume knob on the receiver.

''What's that?'' Dana's voice came from the speaker—
and from the far side of the house. In the next moment,
the woman's voice escalated to a shriek. ''You bastard.
You're broadcasting it!''

A shot reverberated through the house.

"God, no! Alex!" Sara screamed, sick with fear as she charged forward, gun in hand.

Dana had already turned and was coming toward her. "You!" The woman stared at her in wide-eyed astonishment, and maybe the shock was what caused the bullet to go whizzing past Sara's head.

Sara's own fingers were already squeezing the trigger. She fired once, twice, three times, and the woman slumped to the floor.

Leaping past her, Sara sprang into the room.

Alex was sprawled facedown on the floor.

When she set down the gun and knelt at his side, he raised his head, and his eyes were as wide with shock as Dana's had been. "Sara?"

"Alex. Oh Lord, Alex, are you all right?"

"What the hell are you doing here?" he answered. "I was expecting Hempstead."

"The chief had a heart attack. I came instead."

"He sent you? He must not have been thinking too straight."

"Well, he didn't exactly send me. I couldn't leave you here after I heard she was going to kill you. Are you hurt?"

"No. She missed me, thanks to that stunt with the box." He grimaced. "I thought it was Hempstead out there. I was wondering what the hell happened to him."

"I know," she breathed. "I know you had to be playing for time, asking her all those questions."

"Yeah. And I know you could have gotten killed."

"But I didn't," she answered. She was fine. And Alex was fine. Raising her chin, she asked, "If you're not hurt, maybe you'd like to explain when you were going to tell me about Uncle Lee. Or is it Aunt Lacy?"

He used the arm of a chair to lever himself to a sitting

position, then propped his back against the wall. "Give me a minute," he muttered. Gaining his feet, he started across the room.

"Where do you think you're going? Come back here!" she shouted after him, standing up and wedging her hands on her hips.

"After I make sure Dana Eustice isn't coming back in here to shoot us."

Sara suddenly felt all the starch go out of her.

Alex was back in less than a minute. "She's dead."

"I shot her," Sara whispered, her body starting to tremble as the realization hit her.

"Clearly in self-defense. She fired at me and then at you." He slung his arm around her and guided her to the sofa, where he eased her down and turned toward her, rocking her in his arms.

All she could do was try to stop shaking.

She was still clinging to Alex when a uniformed officer found them minutes later. Not the state police this time, but Hempstead's chief deputy.

"Oh God, not again," she moaned. "Are you going to arrest me for shooting Dana Eustice?"

"No. The chief insisted on telling us what happened before they took him to the hospital. He said Dana Eustice confessed to killing Lee Tillman, and she was going to kill you." The man stopped, looked from Alex to her. "And, uh, Tillman is…he had a sex-change operation."

Alex cut him off. "It's on tape. We don't have to talk about it now."

"Yeah, right." The man shook his head. "I guess you've been through enough in the past few days. You can just make a statement down at the station."

"What about the chief?" Sara asked. "Is he going to be okay?"

"They say he is."

"Good," she breathed.

Down at the station, Hempstead's staff listened to Dana Eustice's taped confession to the murders of Emmett Bandy and Tripp Kenney as well as Lee.

Sara could see that the local police were speeding things up for her and Alex, the way the state police had done the day before. And only a couple of hours later, they were free to go.

Feeling almost too limp to walk, Sara let Alex lead her to his SUV. She hardly noticed the ride home until he pulled up in her driveway.

Suddenly her mouth went dry. Back at Dana's house, she'd been ready to confront him. Now that she wasn't charged up with adrenaline, her courage failed.

Still, she had to know where she stood with this man, because it was no longer possible to live with uncertainty. Her lips were parched, and her tongue flicked across them as she turned her face toward him. "Alex?"

"Yeah?"

"What's going to happen? I mean with us."

He didn't answer, and she felt her stomach knot. "You're going back to Baltimore?" she asked.

"I don't know. I mean…"

"Alex, just say it! Whatever it is, say it."

She saw him swallow. In the moments of silence that followed, she felt the earth turn dark and cold. Then he began to speak, and she could hardly focus on what he was saying. "Okay. Here it is. Sara, I've been a fool. I could have gotten you killed. I could have gotten myself killed. I was out of control. Because—" He stopped, and her heart stopped along with him.

"Because?" she managed to say.

"First it was Cindy. I couldn't cope with her betrayal. Then it was you."

Pain flashed through her. "I didn't betray you."

"God, no. That's not what I meant. Not at all. I meant I was afraid to admit the feelings I had for you. Afraid to trust what was happening between us."

"Oh, Alex," she whispered, reaching for him, her arms clenching around him and holding tight.

He had risked telling her some of what was in his heart. She knew she had to take the same risk. Softly she began. "That night in the car with you was a memory I cherished. I never got over you, but I kept telling myself I'd made more of it than I should have. Then, when you came back to St. Stephens, and the feelings for you started building all over again, I was scared, too. Scared that you'd hurt me—because I—I knew you didn't trust me. I knew you thought I was mixed up with what happened to Lee. And, of course, it turned out I was." When he started to speak, she rushed on. "It wasn't just that. I knew that you'd been hurt, and that you didn't want to get involved with anyone. But after they arrested you, I had a lot of time to think, and I realized that I didn't want you to leave me again. I knew that you were worth fighting for. Alex, I love you."

She heard him drag in a breath and let it out. "Sara, I didn't want to love you. I fought tooth and nail against it. But everything that happened drew me closer to you."

She lifted her face and sought his eyes. "I knew you were afraid to trust something good."

"Yes. But then I knew I'd be a fool and a coward to walk away from you. Sara, I do love you. Very much."

"I never thought I'd hear those words from you."

He laughed. "I never thought I could say them. But it's true. And it's true that you gave me back my faith in humanity."

"How?"

"By trusting me. By charging into danger to save me. By making me realize what I'd be losing if I lost you."

"That's how it is for me," she breathed. "Exactly how." She ended the sentence by bringing her lips to his for a long deep kiss filled with warmth and promises.

As he kissed her back, she knew he was making his own promises in return. Promises of deep feelings and caring and commitment—all the things she had longed for in a life mate and was afraid she would never find because she couldn't get over the memories of Alex Shane. But now here he was in her arms again. A dream come true. More than a dream. Reality.

HARLEQUIN ROMANCE®

The rush of falling in love,

Cosmopolitan,
international settings,

Believable, feel-good stories
about today's women

The compelling thrill
of romantic excitement

It could happen to you!

EXPERIENCE
HARLEQUIN ROMANCE!

Available wherever Harlequin Books are sold.

HARLEQUIN®
Live the emotion™

www.eHarlequin.com

HROMDIR04

HARLEQUIN®

American ROMANCE®

Invites *you* to experience lively, heartwarming all-American romances

Every month, we bring you four strong, sexy men, and four women who know what they want—and go all out to get it.

From small towns to big cities, experience a sense of adventure, romance and family spirit—the all-American way!

American ROMANCE

Heart, Home & Happiness

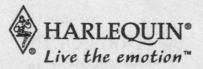 HARLEQUIN®

Live the emotion™

www.eHarlequin.com   HARDIR06

HARLEQUIN®
INTRIGUE®

BREATHTAKING ROMANTIC SUSPENSE

Shared dangers and passions lead to electrifying
romance and heart-stopping suspense!

Every month, you'll meet six new heroes
who are guaranteed to make your spine tingle
and your pulse pound. With them you'll enter
into the exciting world of Harlequin Intrigue—
where your life is on the line
and so is your heart!

THAT'S INTRIGUE—
ROMANTIC SUSPENSE
AT ITS BEST!

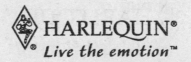

HARLEQUIN®
Live the emotion™

www.eHarlequin.com   INTDIR06

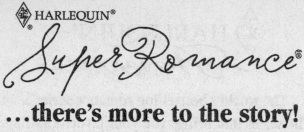

HARLEQUIN®
Super Romance®

...there's more to the story!

Superromance.
A *big* satisfying read about unforgettable characters. Each month we offer *six* very different stories that range from family drama to adventure and mystery, from highly emotional stories to romantic comedies—and much more! Stories about people you'll believe in and care about. Stories too compelling to put down....

Our authors are among today's *best* romance writers. You'll find familiar names and talented newcomers. Many of them are award winners— and you'll see why!

If you want the biggest and best in romance fiction, you'll get it from Superromance!

Exciting, Emotional, Unexpected...

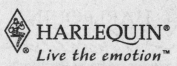

HARLEQUIN®
Live the emotion™

HARLEQUIN®
Presents~

The world's bestselling romance series...
The series that brings you your favorite authors,
month after month:

Helen Bianchin...Emma Darcy
Lynne Graham...Penny Jordan
Miranda Lee...Sandra Marton
Anne Mather...Carole Mortimer
Susan Napier...Michelle Reid

and many more uniquely talented authors!

Wealthy, powerful, gorgeous men...
Women who have feelings just like your own...
The stories you love, set in exotic, glamorous locations...

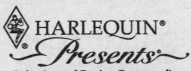

HARLEQUIN®
Presents~
Seduction and Passion Guaranteed!

www.eHarlequin.com   HPDIR104

Harlequin® Historical
Historical Romantic Adventure!

*Imagine a time of chivalrous
knights and unconventional ladies,
roguish rakes and impetuous
heiresses, rugged cowboys
and spirited frontierswomen—
these rich and vivid tales will
capture your imagination!*

*Harlequin Historical . . .
they're too good to miss!*

passionate powerful provocative love stories

Silhouette Desire delivers strong heroes, spirited heroines and compelling love stories.

Desire features your favorite authors, including

Annette Broadrick, Diana Palmer, Maureen Child and Brenda Jackson.

Passionate, powerful and provocative romances *guaranteed!*

For superlative authors, sensual stories and sexy heroes, choose Silhouette Desire.

passionate powerful provocative love stories

Visit Silhouette Books at www.eHarlequin.com   SDGEN06